FIC   Carroll, Jonathan, 1949-

Voice of our shadow

DATE			

VOICE
OF OUR
SHADOW

ALSO BY JONATHAN CARROLL

The Land of Laughs

JONATHAN CARROLL

VOICE
OF OUR
SHADOW

THE VIKING PRESS
NEW YORK

Copyright © 1983 by Jonathan Carroll
All rights reserved
First published in 1983 by The Viking Press
625 Madison Avenue, New York, N.Y. 10022
Published simultaneously in Canada by
Penguin Books Canada Limited

LIBRARY OF CONGRESS CATALOGING IN PUBLICATION DATA
Carroll, Jonathan, 1949–
Voice of our shadow.
I.Title.
PS3553.A7646V6   1982   813'.54   82-70560
ISBN 0-670-49240-X   AACR2

Grateful acknowledgment is made to Viking Penguin Inc.
for permission to reprint a selection from *Self-Portrait in a
Convex Mirror* by John Ashbery. Copyright © 1972, 1973,
1974, 1975 by John Ashbery.

Printed in the United States of America
Set in CRT Electra

FOR MY FATHER—
" 'Then it is yours. I pray you accept it.'
'My pleasure, sir. My very great pleasure.' "

A look of glass stops you
And you walk on shaken: was I the perceived?
Did they notice me, this time, as I am,
Or is it postponed again?
John Ashbery, "As One Put Drunk into
the Packet Boat"

PART ONE

I

Formori, Greece

At night here I often dream of my parents. They are good dreams and I wake happy and refreshed, although nothing very important happens in them. We will be sitting on the porch in summer, drinking iced tea and watching our scottie dog, Jordan, lope across the front yard. Although we talk, the words are pale and dreamy, unimportant. It makes no difference—we are all very glad to be there, even my brother, Ross.

Now and then Mother laughs or throws her arms out in those great swoops and arcs when she talks—her most familiar gesture. My father smokes a cigarette, inhaling so deeply that I once asked him when I was young if the smoke went down into his legs.

As is true with so many couples, my parents' temperaments were diametrically opposed. Mother ate life as fast as she could get her hands on it. Dad, on the other hand, was clear and predictable and forever the straight man to her passion and shenanigans. I think the only great sadness in their relationship for him was knowing that although she loved him in a warm, companionable way, she went all-out in adoring her two sons. Originally she had wanted to have five children, but both my brother and I had such difficult births the doctor told her having another child would be a deadly risk. She compensated in the end by pouring the love for those five kids into the two of us.

Dad was a veterinarian; still *is* a veterinarian. He'd had a successful practice in Manhattan when they were first married, but gave it up to move to the country right after his first son was born. He wanted his children to have a yard to play in and the safety to come and go as they pleased any time of the day.

As with everything else in her life, my mother pounced on the new house and tore it limb from limb. New paint inside and out, new wallpaper, floors stripped and sealed, leaks stopped ... When she was done she had created a solid, amiable place with more than enough room, light, warmth, and security to assure each of us this was a home as well as a house.

All that and two little boys to raise. Later she said those first two years in the house were her happiest. Everywhere she went, either someone or something needed her, and that is what she thrived on. With one boy in her arms and another clinging to her skirt, she telephoned, cooked, and hammered the house and our new life there into submission. It took a few years, but when she was done, things both worked *and* gleamed. Ross was starting school, she'd taught me how to read, and every meal she put on the table was tasty and different.

When she felt we were all taken care of, she went out and bought the dog for us.

My brother, Ross, quickly turned into an eager, curious kid who, at five years old, was already supremely naughty. The kind who does ghastly things but is constantly being forgiven because people think the act was either accidental or cute.

When he was a toddler he used to scour the house looking for new things to poke into or take apart. Over the years he moved through Tinkertoys, Silly Putty, and Erector Sets like an express train. Much against my dad's wishes, Mother bought him a wood-burning kit for his sixth birthday. He used it properly for a couple of weeks, spelling his name on any piece of scrap wood he could find. Then he spelled ROSS LENNOX on an oak armchair. Mother spanked him and threw the burner away. She was like that—very determined, and sure that the only way to raise children was to love them all the time, notwithstanding the necessary smack now and then when they deserved it. No excuses, no apologies—if you did it, you got hit. Five minutes later she was hugging you again and would do anything in the world for you. I must have understood her way very early in life, because I was rarely hit. But not Ross; God, not Ross. The reason I'm mentioning the episode is that it was the first time the two of them really knocked heads over something. Ross burned the chair, Mother spanked him and threw the thing in the garbage. When she was gone he took it out of the garbage and carefully burned holes in the bottoms of her expensive new leather boots.

She discovered them an hour later and, to my horror, asked me if I'd done it. Me! I was the dullard who watched these titans with awe and trembling. No, I hadn't done it. Of course she knew that, but needed to hear it from me before she took action. Marching into Ross's room, she found him sitting calmly on the bed reading a comic book. Just as calmly, she went over to his dresser and picked up his favorite model airplane. Lifting the burner out of her apron pocket, she plugged it into the wall and, in front of his astonished eyes, burned holes through the middle of both wings. He wailed, the room stank horribly, and those black, wispy threads of singed plastic floated everywhere. When she was done she put the plane back on the dresser and walked out of the room, winner and still champion.

She won that time, but as he grew older, Ross became increasingly more clever and wily; their duel continued, but on an equal level.

What happened was, my brother had inherited her vitality and appetite for life, but rather than desiring everything, as she did, he preferred specific courses in huge servings. If life was a massive feast, he only wanted the pâté, but he wanted all of it.

And manipulate? There was no one who could do it better. I was the world's biggest pushover and no challenge at all, but in the short span of three months one summer he got me to: break the window in my father's study, throw a rock point-blank at a beehive (while he stood inside the house watching), give him my allowance so he'd protect me from God, who, he said, was always on the brink of throwing me into hell for my evil six-year-old behavior. My father had an old copy of *The Inferno* with Doré's illustrations, and Ross showed it to me one afternoon to let me know what I was in for if I didn't continue to pay him protection money. The pictures were both so horrific and so engrossing that I needed no prompting after that (and for the next few weeks, until the spell wore off) to take the book down on my own and marvel at what I'd just barely avoided with my brother's help.

I was certainly his prime chump, but he could throw his lasso around most people. He knew how to work my mother so she'd let him stay home from school, my father so he'd take us to a Yankee game or a drive-in movie. Naturally he got caught once in a while and was hit or punished, but his record (what he called his "won-lost record") was astounding compared to most other kids'.

In comparison, I was the archangel Gabriel. I think I made my bed from the day I could toddle, and in my endless prayers at night I asked God to bless everyone I could think of, including the Barnum & Bailey circus.

I had a hamster in a silver-colored cage, a Lone Ranger rug, and college pennants on my walls. I kept all my pencils sharpened and my Hardy Boys books in strict alphabetical order. In answer to this, one of the many things Ross liked to do was come into my room and dive-bomb my bed. He'd spread his arms out as far as they would go and hit it at top speed. Often one of the wooden support slats groaned or even broke, and the pillow would fly up in the air from shock. I'd whine, and he'd hee-hee with delight. But having him in there was a great treat, so I never complained too loudly. He once put half a dead cat on my pillow with a little baseball cap on its head, and I never told a soul. I tried to pretend it was a special secret we had between us.

His room was the opposite of mine, but ten times more wonderful, always. I admit it. Everything was in an uproar, from sneakers on the desk to a radio under his mattress. He and my mother had world wars about his room, but it stayed his way three quarters of the time, regardless of her hair-pulling or threats. The most amazing thing about it was the variety of stuff he'd accumulated.

None of those college pennants for him. He'd gotten hold of an immense movie poster advertising *Godzilla*. That covered one wall in flames, blood, and lightning. On another was a tattered Albanian flag my father'd brought back from the war. On the bookshelves were a complete collection of *Famous Monsters* magazine, a leprous-looking stuffed skunk, all of the Oz books, and several of those old cartoon-like cast-iron banks that are so popular in antique shops these days.

He loved to go to the town dump and spend hours with a long metal pole, rummaging through piles, flipping aside things that he wanted to take home. He'd found a porcelain snuff box there, a railroad clock with no hands, a book on paper dolls that had been published in 1873.

I remember all this because some time ago I woke up in the middle of the night after having had one of those remarkably clear dreams; the kind where everything you experience is in such cold, clear light that you feel out of place in the real world once you wake up. Anyway, my dream took place in his old room, and when I came awake, I grabbed a pencil and paper and wrote down a list of all the things I'd seen.

If a boy's room is an out-of-focus picture of what he'll later turn out to be in life, Ross would have been . . . an antique dealer? An eccentric? Something unforeseeable but very special, I think. What I remember best was lying on his bed (whenever he'd permit me in the room—I had to knock before I entered) and letting my eyes run over his shelves and walls and things. Feeling as if I were in some land or on a planet that was impossibly far from our house, from my life. And when I'd seen everything for the hundredth time, I would look at Ross and be delighted that however foreign or strange or cruel, he was my brother and we shared a house, a name, our blood.

His taste changed as he got older, but that only meant things became more wacky. For a while he was obsessed with old typewriters. At any one time he would have three or four of them lying around in a thousand pieces on his desk. He joined a club for antique typewriter collectors and for months wrote and received hundreds of letters. Swapping parts, getting and giving repair tips . . . Once in a while a strange, mossy voice from Perry, Oklahoma, or Hickory, North Carolina, would call and ask for him. Ross talked to these other fanatics with the poise and assurance of a forty-year-old master repairman.

From typewriters he moved on to antique kites, then Shar-Pei dogs, followed closely by Edgar Cayce and the Rosicrucians.

It sounds as if he was a burgeoning wunderkind, and to a degree he was, but away from his obsessions Ross was sullen and sly as a splinter. He constantly locked the door to his room and was consequently suspected by my parents of doing all kinds of "things" in there. I kept telling them he did it to get their goat, but they didn't listen to me.

For any number of reasons, he would have a battle royal with my mother two or three times a week. With her hair-trigger temper, he knew how easy it was to make her mad (chew with his mouth open, not wipe his feet . . .), but that didn't satisfy him. When he was in the mood, he wanted her tied in fiery knots, raging, stumbling from a fury so blind she actually bumped into things.

I gather it's not uncommon for families to be at one an-other's throats during the kids' so-called formative years, but what happened in our family was that as Mother lost more and more ground to Ross, it made her increasingly wary of both of us. I was a coward and took to the hills whenever I felt her temperature rising, but I couldn't always escape. The fallout from her flashes of anger often hurt me, and I couldn't believe the unfairness of the world. I knew I was a happy, normal little boy. I knew, too, that my brother was everything but. I knew he drove my mother nuts, and I read-ily understood why she blew her top at him. But what never made sense to me was how I got dragged into their often brutal melees and ended up being slapped or screamed at or punished for no reason at all.

Did that scar me for life and make me hate all mothers I've met since? Not at all. It scared and awed me to see Ross act that way, but I was also the most captive member of his audience. Even including the occasional whack, I wouldn't have traded living on the outskirts of hurricane country for anything in the world.

Soon he was stealing whatever he could lay his hands on. He was a premier thief, due in large part to chutzpah. He was constantly stopped in stores and asked where he was going with that watch (book, lighter . . .). With a guileless, uncomprehending look, he would say he was just bringing it

JONATHAN CARROLL

over there to his mother. After being stared down by Ross,
the salesperson would apologize for being so gruff with him.
Five minutes later Ross would have the thing in his pocket
and be out on the street.

Once, he had a fight with my mother the day after
Christmas and told her he'd stolen every one of the presents
he'd given us. She erupted, but my calm father—saddened
but used to it by then—just asked which store they'd come
from. Ross wouldn't say, and we were off on the carousel
again.

Five days later my parents went out to a New Year's Eve
party and made Ross baby-sit for me. Ten minutes after
they were out the door, he dared me to slide down the banister with my eyes closed. I'd gone a couple of feet before I
felt something hideous and burning on the back of my
hand. I threw both arms up, knocking away the cigarette
he'd been singeing me with. Losing my balance, I fell over
the side and landed on my arm, which instantly snapped in
two places. All I remember besides the pain is Ross's face
right up next to mine, telling me again and again I'd better
keeping my fucking little mouth shut about this.

Was I a fool? Yes. Should I have screamed bloody mur-
der? Yes. Did I want my brother to love me just a little? Yes.

2

When he was fifteen Ross changed his image and became a
tough guy. Leather jacket with a thousand zippers and
chrome studs, a bone-handled switchblade knife from Italy,
a tube of Brylcreem hair goop on the shelf in the bathroom.

He hung around with a bunch of dimwits who, instead of talking, smoked Marlboros and spat on the ground. The leader of this pack was named Bobby Hanley, who, although short and skinny as a car antenna, had a nasty reputation. It was assumed that anyone who messed with him was out of his mind.

The first time I ever saw Bobby was at a high school basketball game. I was eleven, and because I was still in elementary school, I didn't know who he was. I'd come to the game with Ross (who'd been forced into taking me by my parents), but he ditched me seconds after we got there. I'd looked around frantically for someone to sit with, but it seemed as if everyone was a stranger. I ended up standing by the main door. A few minutes into the game an old janitor who I knew was named Vince came in and stood next to me. He had one of those long wooden brooms in his hand; every time our side scored he'd stamp it on the ground. We started talking, and I felt more comfortable. It was very pleasant, and I started thinking about how great it would be when I was in high school and could come to these games all the time with my friends.

A few minutes before the end of the first quarter the door whacked open and a bunch of tough guys sashayed in. Vince muttered something about "little turds," and since I didn't know anything, I nodded.

They walked right up to the out-of-bounds line and stood there, checking out the crowd, ignoring the game completely. Then one of them took out a pack of cigarettes and lit up. He threw the match on the floor. Vince walked up and told him there was no smoking in the gym. Bobby Hanley didn't even look his way. Instead, he took a long, slow drag and said, "Blow it out your ass, Pop."

I couldn't believe it! The even more astonishing thing was, Vince mumbled something, but walked back to the door.

A few of Hanley's crew snickered, but none of them had

11

the nerve to light up too. Standing next to me, Vince cursed and kept moving his hands around on the top of the broom. I didn't know what to do. How could this kid get away with that? What kind of crazy power did he have?

The quarter ended as Bobby smoked his cigarette down to the brown filter. When he was done he dropped it on the hardwood floor and ground it out with his boot heel. I watched his foot move back and forth. Much too loudly I said, "What a big jerk."

"Hey, Bobby, numb-nuts over there called you a jerk."

I froze.

"Who did?"

"The little fuck over there by the door. The orange sweater."

"A jerk, huh?"

I wouldn't look up. I wanted to close my eyes, but I didn't. I saw the lower half of Hanley push through his entourage and walk toward me. He grabbed my ear and pulled it up next to his mouth.

"You called me a jerk?"

"Leave the kid alone, Hanley."

Still holding me tight, Bobby told the janitor to fuck off.

"I asked you a question, scumbag. I'm a jerk?"

"You're not supposed to smoke in the gym. Ow!"

"Says who, scumbag? Who's going to stop me?"

Silence. People moved around us. I was so scared and ashamed. I had no guts. Everyone in the world was looking at me. No one knew who I was, but that made no difference. Whoever I was, I was a chickenshit. Hanley was slowly tearing my ear off. I was sure I could hear little things coming apart in there: muscles from bone, soft little membranes and hairs like the thinnest spiderwebs ... His friends stood around us in a semicircle, delighted to be part of the scene.

"Listen to me, scumbag." He stepped forward and planted his heel on top of my sneaker. He shoved down on it; I yelped as the pain soared up through my body. I started to cry. "Scumbag's crying now. Why're you crying?"

Where was Vince? Where was my father? My brother? My brother—ha! Even then, in the midst of that scene, I knew if Ross had been around he would've laughed himself sick.

"Hey, Bobby, Madeleine's waiting for you."

I looked directly at him for the first time. He was much shorter than I'd thought. Who was Madeleine? Was he going to go away now?

"Look, scummy, don't you ever let me see you around here again, understand? 'Cause if I do, I'm going to cut your fuckin' eyes out with this." He pulled a beer opener out of his pocket and pressed it hard against my nose. I remember how warm it was. I nodded as best I could, and he shoved me away. I cracked my head on a bleacher and went down like a stone in water. When I looked up again the whole gang of them was gone.

For months afterward I skulked around school like a haunted shadow. When I crept into the building in the morning, I checked every corridor, every classroom, every bathroom before I went in or out, just in case he was there. I knew the chances of his ever being in the elementary school were remote, but I wasn't about to tempt fate.

I told no one about it, especially not Ross. At night I sometimes dreamed I was running as fast as I could on a soft rubber road chased by a gigantic dancing beer opener.

Nothing ever happened, so by the time Ross and Bobby teamed up a year later, I felt only a sharp cut of fear when I saw them together for the first time.

The final indignity was that when Bobby came over to our house for the first time he didn't even recognize me. When Ross said by way of introduction, "That's my shitty little brother," Bobby only smiled and said, "How're you doin', man?"

How was I *doing?* I wanted to tell him . . . No, I wanted to demand that he recognize me. Me, scumbag, the one he'd scared so badly for huge months of my life.

But I didn't. Later I got up the guts to remind him of that first meeting. He snapped his fingers as if he'd forgotten to buy shoelaces. "Yeah, sure, I thought I knew your face." And that was all.

Naturally the longer he hung around with Ross, the more I liked him. He was very funny and had a kind of sensitivity that enabled him, like my brother, to see right through to a person's strengths and weaknesses. He used this ability to his own benefit about ninety percent of the time, but once in a while he did something so extraordinarily nice you were knocked for a loop.

Just before my thirteenth birthday the three of us were in a stationery store and I wistfully mentioned how much I wanted a certain model of the aircraft carrier *Forrestal* they had on the shelves. When my big day arrived, Bobby came over to the house and handed me the model, gift-wrapped. "Shit, man, did you ever try to steal something that big? It's fucking hard!" I made the model more carefully than any other. I showed it to him only after I'd spent hours painting and sanding it to perfection. He nodded appreciatively and told Ross I knew what I was doing. That year Ross's present to me was a small rubber doll of a woman in a bathing suit whose breasts popped out from behind the suit whenever you squeezed her stomach.

I think Hanley originally liked my brother because Ross was very smart. School was easy for him, and he often ended up doing Bobby's homework for him, although the latter was a grade ahead.

However, I'm not trying to say that was the only reason for their friendship. When he felt like it, my brother not only could charm the birds out of the trees but could make anyone in the world laugh. He wasn't a clown, but among his many gifts was an acute sensitivity to your likes and dislikes, as well as the ability to send you howling. Since Hanley was the undisputed king of the high school, Ross cased the scene before making his move. He decided to become the older boy's court jester. He wasn't tough like the others in the gang, but he was damned shrewd! After only a short time there were a million punks in town who wanted to beat Ross to smithereens, but they left him alone because they all knew he was safely under Bobby's dangerous wing.

In a different environment who knows what might have happened to the two of them. Both Bobby and Ross had an élan, the magician's touch; that special rare ability to turn cruelty into pink handkerchiefs and kindness into thin air.

The two of them palled around more and more, but my parents didn't mind because Bobby was quiet and courteous when he came over for dinner. Also, he appeared to be having a very good effect. At home, Ross wasn't half as nasty or selfish as he had been. He didn't go out of his way to be friendly or helpful, but there were faint glimmerings that he might have turned a corner and was heading in some kind of right direction.

The night before Ross died, Bobby slept over at our house. Ross was very excited because he had been given a twelve-gauge shotgun for his birthday a few days before. My father loved to shoot trap and skeet and had promised to teach us the sport when we reached sixteen.

Bobby had guns of his own, but this one was a beauty he could appreciate. They allowed me to stay in the room with them that evening, even when Ross pulled out the new dirty magazines he'd stolen from the candy store. They smoked almost a full pack of cigarettes and spent the hours talking about the girls at school, different kinds of cars, what Bobby would do when he graduated.

I slept on a hassock that opened out into a bed. Ross let me do that, too. Hours later, I jerked awake when I felt something thick and warm and gooey on my face. Both of them were standing by my bed, and in the dim light I saw

Ross tipping a bottle of something over me. I opened my mouth to protest and tasted the heavy sweetness of maple syrup. By that time it was all over me. There was nothing I could do but get up and bump my way out of the room, followed by their pleased laughter. I washed out my pajama top in the sink as best I could, so that my mother would never know about it. Then I took a long shower in the dark.

When I awoke the next day, I felt feverish and uncomfortable. The strong morning sunlight poured through the windows and over me like an extra, unnecessary blanket.

After I brushed my teeth, I went to Ross's room and knocked on the door. When there was no answer I cautiously pushed it open. There were wooden bunk beds in both our rooms. I saw Ross hanging over the edge of the top one, busily talking to Bobby, who was lying on his back with his hands behind his head.

"What do you want, asshole? More syrup?"

Bobby fanned a fly away from his nose and yawned. Last night's joke was last night, and now it was time for something new.

"You know, Ross, if you could sneak that shotgun out of the house, we could go down to the river and pick off a few seagulls. I hate those fucking birds."

We lived half a mile from a river. It was a place where you went in the summer when there was nothing else to do, or if you were lucky enough to have convinced a girl to go "swimming" there with you. Since the water was so brown and polluted, you never swam—as soon as you got your towels down on the beach you started necking.

To get to the water you had to cross railroad tracks. You did it carefully and stepped ridiculously high over anything that looked even vaguely suspicious: down there somewhere on the ground was the *third rail* and you knew that if you ever so much as touched it you would be instantly electrocuted.

Bobby and Ross had been down to the tracks before with guns. In fact, Ross was the only other member of the gang who'd had the "guts" to shoot at passing cattle cars with one of Bobby's many rifles. They were never caught.

My parents went shopping that morning, so there was no problem taking the gun out of the house. Ross slid it back into its cardboard box, and that was that for camouflage. They allowed me to tag along on the threat that if I said anything about it afterward they'd boil me in oil.

When we got down to the tracks Bobby told Ross to get the gun out—he wanted to take a couple of shots. I could see Ross wanted to shoot first; a peeved, mean look swept across his face. But it was gone in an instant. He handed the gun over, along with a bunch of red and brassy-gold shells he had stuffed in his back pocket. The only thing he had left was the empty box; he threw that at me.

The sun was hot, and I peeled off my T-shirt. When it was halfway over my head, I heard the *pof* of the first shot and an instantaneous crash of glass somewhere.

"Holy shit, Bobby! You think you hit the station?" Ross's voice was high and scared.

"I'll be fucked if I know, man." He reloaded and shot off in another direction. I put my hands over my ears and looked at the ground. I was already petrified, and things had just begun.

"Ross, baby, this is one honey of a gun. I can tell already. Let's go, man."

We walked twelve or fifteen feet apart. Bobby, Ross, then me. That's very important, as you'll see in a moment. Bobby held the shotgun down at his side, barrel toward the ground. I saw it out of the corner of my eye. It was dull blue and the railroad tracks under our feet were hot silver as we stepped gingerly over them. The light everywhere burned my eyes and made me squint. I wished to God I was home. What were they going to do now? What would happen if they were in the mood for something unnecessary and vicious, like shooting at cattle as they moved slowly by in those slat-ted red and brown freight cars, already on their way to the slaughterhouse? I hated the gun, I hated my great fear, I hated my brother and his friend. But they would never, ever know that.

We were moving at the same pace, our legs lifting and falling at the same time. Then Ross stumbled on something and fell straight forward. I heard an angry buzz like an out-board motor, the gravel skittering away from under my brother's sneaker. His shoulder touched the third rail, and his head twisted around on his neck. There was a loud hum, a sharp hiss and snap. His face twisted up and up and up into an impossible, irretrievable smile.

3

Why am I lying? Why am I already leaving out a part of this story that is so necessary? What difference does it make now? All right. Before I go on, here's a piece of the puzzle I've been hiding behind my back.

Bobby had an older sister named Lee. At eighteen she was the most stunning girl you'd ever want to see. By the time Ross and Bobby became close friends, she had been out of school for a few years, but people still talked about her because she was really incredible.

She'd been captain of the cheerleaders, a member of the Pep Club and the Gourmet Club. I knew all of this by heart because Ross had a high school yearbook from when she graduated, and as is so often the case with the prettiest girl in school, it seemed as if her face was on every other page:

cartwheeling, being crowned Prom Queen, smiling magnificently at us from behind an armload of books. How many times had I devoured those pictures? Hundreds? A thousand? A lot.

What I didn't understand until later was that part of her special aura came from pure sensuality. I didn't know if she was "fast," because my only authority on her was my brother, who contended he'd had her a million times, but even the most innocent of those pictures gave off an aroma of sexiness as strong as the smell of fresh baked bread.

Ross's birthday present when I turned twelve was to teach me how to masturbate. Part of the gift was a three-month-old copy of *Gent* magazine, but from the first I could only climax if I thought of real women. The zeppelin breasts and sex-crazed expressions of those pinup girls scared me more than turned me on. No, my idea of sexual frenzy was the photograph of Lee Hanley doing a jump cheer at a football game that had somehow caught a delicious smidgen of her underpants while she was in mid-flight.

Let me say, though, that I'd fallen in love with her long before I learned to play with myself, so the first time I used her as my fantasy woman I felt rotten, because I knew I'd somehow let her down, regardless of the fact I'd never said two words to her. But that guilt was short-lived, because my twelve-year-old penis was anxious to get on with business, so I continued to ravish her picture with my hungry eyes and myself with a jumpy hand.

Sometimes I'd get completely carried away, and looking at the ceiling as I felt my body blast off into the stratosphere, I'd start to call her name again and again. *Lee Hanley! Oh! Leeee!* Although I tried to waltz myself around only when I was sure no one else was home, I made the mistake of not checking one afternoon, and that oversight was disastrous.

Bermuda shorts down at my knees, the school yearbook propped comfortably on my chest, I had started singing my

Lee song when the door suddenly flew open and Ross appeared.

"*I caught you!* Lee Hanley, huh? You're jerking off to Lee Hanley? Boy, wait'll Bobby hears this! He's going to chop you into hamburger. Hey, what've you got there? That's *my* yearbook! Gimme that!" He snatched it out of my hand and looked at the picture. "Jeez, wait'll I tell Bobby, man. Shit, I'd hate to be you." His face was pure triumph.

From that moment on, the taunts and torture began and didn't end for more than a year. That night I pulled down the bedspread and found a photograph taped to my pillow: a mutilated body on a battlefield with a soldier looking at it indifferently. In blood-red ink the soldier was labeled *Bobby,* and I was the corpse.

A lot of that sort of thing went on, but the most frightening moments were when Ross would casually say to Bobby, "Want to know what my brother does, Bobby? Wait'll you hear this one, the little pig!" Looking straight at me, a gleam smeared across his face, he'd pause for millenniums, making me wish I was either in Sumatra or dead, or both. Inevitably he'd finish by saying, "He picks his nose," or something equally mean and true, but nothing compared to "it," and I could breathe easily again.

It ran in cycles; at times I was hopeful he'd forgotten. But like a bat flying through the window, it would suddenly be there again, right on you, days or weeks later, and he'd have me squirming and twisting at the drop of his hat. When we were alone he would tell me what a sludge I was to jerk off to a friend's *sister.* He was as convincing as any angry, unforgiving priest.

Probably because the torment increased, the image of Lee Hanley's underpants became the sexiest thing in the world, and they became my one and only fantasy. I masturbated at all times of the day; my high point was probably the time I came while sitting perfectly still at a junior high school assembly where a Cherokee Indian demonstrated tribal war dances.

I was a fool. I gave Ross my allowance, did his chores for him, brought him snacks at the snap of his fingers. Once, I even realized that what I'd been doing was a kind of compliment to Lee, but when I tried explaining that to Ross, he closed his eyes and flicked his wrist at me as if I were a fly on his hand.

What really happened the day he died was this: as we were crossing the railroad tracks together, Ross's anger flared at Bobby for having taken his shotgun away. Halfway to the other platform, he casually asked his friend how many times a week he beat off.

"I don't know. Every day, I guess. That is, if I'm not gettin' any from some chick. Why? How 'bout you?"

My brother's voice went up a notch. "About the same. Do you ever think of anyone when you do it?"

My face tightened, and I almost stopped moving.

"Sure, what do you think I do, count to a hundred? What's with you, Ross? You gone pervert or something?"

"Naah, I was just thinking. Do you know who Joe thinks about when he does it?"

"Joey? You beating your meat already, boy? Shame! You know how old I was when I first started doing it? About three!" He laughed.

I could only look at my feet. I knew it was coming; Ross was about to open the door on my blackest secret and there was nothing I could do about it.

"Okay, so spill it. Who do you think about, Joe? Suzanne Pleshette?"

Before Ross could answer, a high train whistle hooted frighteningly down the track. At that moment I did something I'd never done before. Shouting "No!" I shoved Ross as hard as I could. So help me God, I was so afraid of what he was going to say I'd totally forgotten where we were.

"Holy shit, Ross, a train's coming!" Without looking our way, Bobby charged ahead toward the other side of the tracks. My brother fell. I stood still and watched. Yes.

4

I was so shocked by what had happened I couldn't say anything. A few days later I was too afraid to speak.

Conveniently, as far as people were concerned (including Bobby, who testified that the sound of the train whistle must have scared Ross into stumbling), it was simply a tragic accident.

My mother went mad. A week after the funeral she stood at the bottom of the staircase and started screaming incoherently to my dead brother to get up and go to school. She had to be institutionalized. I began shaking and was put on heavy doses of tranquilizer, which made me feel as if I were floating in blue space.

When they decided to keep my mother in the hospital, my father took me to dinner. Neither of us ate anything. Halfway through the meal he pushed the plates aside and took hold of both my hands.

"Joe, son, it's going to be just you and me for a while now, and we've got some tough times ahead of us."

I nodded and was for the first time on the brink of telling him everything, every bit of it. Then he looked at me, and I saw big clear tears on his face.

"I'm crying, Joe, because of your brother, and because I already miss your mama very much. It makes me feel as if parts of my body had been ripped off. I'm telling you that because I think you can understand and because I'm going to need you to help me be strong. I'll help you and you'll help me, okay? You're the best boy a man could have, and we're not going to let anything get us or pull us down from now on. Not anything! Right?"

I saw Bobby only two or three times after Ross died. When the school year ended he enlisted in the Marines. He left town at the end of June, but stories trickled back about him. Apparently he turned out to be a very good soldier. He stayed in the service for four years. By the time he returned I was a freshman in college.

In my sophomore year I came home for a long weekend. On Saturday night I had a dreary argument with my father about what I was going to do with "my future." I left the house in a huff and went to a bar in town to drown my angst in beer.

Along about the third one, someone sat down next to me at the bar and touched my elbow. I was watching television and ignored it. Whoever it was touched me again, and annoyed, I looked over. It was Bobby. His hair was very long, and he had a Fu Manchu mustache that grew down and off his square chin. He smiled and patted my arm.

"My God, Bobby!"

"How are you doin' there, Joe College?"

He kept smiling, and I realized, with some relief, he was very stoned.

"How's college, Joe?"

"Great, Bobby. But how are you?"

"Good, man. Everything is very cool."

"Yeah? Well, what are you doing? I mean, uh, what kind of work are you into?"

"Listen, Joe, I've been wanting to rap with you for like a

long time, you know? There's a lot to talk about between us, you know?"

His face was thin and tired, and there was an uncertainty that said he'd banged around through the years without having found much of anything. I felt very sorry for him, but knew there was little I could do. His hand was on my shoulder, so I reached over and took it, wanting him to know that in a strange way he was still an important part of me.

I've mentioned before how he had always been very sensitive. Touching his hand like that set something off. He snatched it away, and his look changed abruptly. The snaky, malicious Bobby Hanley who'd held a beer opener to my face rushed back. Rage flew up into his eyes like a small bird hitting a window. I winced and tried to smile us back to a moment ago.

"Hey, man, I got a question for you. You ever go out to your brother's grave? Huh? You ever go there and give Ross flowers or anything?"

"I—"

"You bullshit! You don't, man, and I know it! I'm out there all the fucking time, do you know that? The guy was the greatest friend I ever had in the world! You're his own little brother and you don't do squat for him. No wonder he thought you were a little pussy. You shithead!" He wrenched himself off the stool and dug into his pocket for money. Coming up with a dollar bill that had been crumpled into a small green ball, he threw it on the counter. It rolled until it fell over the other edge. "You think I don't know about you, Joe? You think I don't know how you feel about Ross? Well, let me tell you something, man. He was a king, and don't ever forget that. He was a fucking *king.* You—Christ, all you are is a scumbag!"

He walked out of the bar without looking back. I wanted to go after him and tell him he was wrong. I waited, pretending I was trying to think of what I'd say when I caught up with him. Say? I didn't have anything to tell him; there was nothing more *to* say.

A month later I wrote a short story entitled "Wooden Pajamas" for a creative-writing class I was taking. The teacher had encouraged us umpteen times to write from our own experience. Because I was still shaken by the meeting with Bobby, I decided to follow the advice and try driving some of the guilt monsters away by writing a story about Bobby, Ross, and their gang.

The problem was what to write. In my first attempt, I tried describing the time they planned to rob the American Legion post of all its guns, only to be cheated out of the chance when the building burned down the night before the caper was to be pulled off. I say I tried writing about it, but all I came up with was a bunch of crap. I realized I didn't know how to approach my brother and his world. He and all he'd been had flowed through my veins for so long that when I stopped to think about who and what he was, I drew a blank. I knew what colors he was, but since I couldn't separate them, they all merged into a big white blank. Just try to describe the color white to someone beyond saying it's all colors in one.

I tried a first-person narrator—a girl who'd been jilted by one of the guys. That didn't work, so I tried being one of their parents. Absolutely nothing. Next I filled three sheets of paper with Ross and Bobby stories. Some of them made me laugh; others made me guilty or sad. Remembering everything made me obsessed with the idea of getting a bit of their world down on paper. Nothing was going to stop me.

It's funny, but in the beginning I never once thought of making something up and using my brother and his gang as characters in *my* story. Ross had been such a strong presence in my life and had done so many wild things that I'd never considered upstaging him with an action or thought that came strictly from my own head. Yet that's what happened. While driving across campus one Saturday night, I saw a bunch of tough guys strutting down Main Street, all duded up for a big night on the town.

How many times had I watched my brother brush his long hair into a perfect shining swirl, slap on a gallon of English Leather cologne, and wink at himself in the bathroom mirror when he was done? "Looking good, Joe. Your brother is look-ing good!"

I thought about it for a while and, sitting down at the typewriter one afternoon, opened the story with those same words addressed to an adoring little brother who sat on the edge of the bathtub watching him prepare for . . . I had no idea of where to go from there.

It took me two weeks to write. It was about a bunch of toughs in a small town who are getting ready to go to a big party at a girl's house. Each boy has a little section of the story, and in turn tells you about their lives and what he thinks will happen tonight when the party gets going up at Brenda's.

I never worked on anything so hard in my life. I loved it. I laid each story on top of the previous one as gently as if I were building a house of cards. I shifted them around and around incessantly for best effect and made my teacher mad because I turned the assignment in a week after it was due. When I was done, however, I knew I'd written something good, maybe even special. I was really proud of it.

My teacher liked it, too, and suggested I submit it to a magazine. I did; over the months it made the rounds of all the major and minor places. Finally *Timepiece*—circulation 700—took it. Payment was only two contributor's copies, but I was overjoyed. I had the cover of that issue framed and put it up on the wall in front of my desk.

Three months later a theatrical producer in New York

called and asked if I'd be willing to sell him the world rights
to the story for two thousand dollars. Amazed, I was on the
verge of saying yes when I remembered stories of writers
being gypped out of carloads of money by conniving pro-
ducers; so I told him to call me back in a few days. I found a
copy of *Writer's Market* in the college library and got the
names and telephone numbers of four or five literary agents.
I explained the situation to the first one I called and asked
her what I should do. By the end of the conversation she'd
agreed to represent me, and when the man called back from
New York, I told him to arrange everything through her.

You know what happens when you sell a story to someone: they push it and pull it and turn it inside out. When
they're done eviscerating it ("shaping it up," they like to call
it), they put it in front of the public with a line in the program that reads something like "Based on an original short
story by Joseph Lennox."

The producer of the play, a tall man with bright-red hair
named Phil Westberg, called me just after he'd bought the
story and politely asked how I would approach it as a play. I
didn't know anything, so I said something dumb and forget-
table, but he didn't want to hear what I had to say anyway,
because he had it all planned out. He began to tell me his
plan, and at one point I took the telephone receiver away
from my ear and looked at it as if it were an eggplant. He
was talking about "Wooden Pajamas," but they weren't *my*
pajamas. The short story began in a bathroom, the play at
the big party, which instantly cut out about four thousand
words of my work. The protagonist in the play was thrown
in as an afterthought in the story. But Westberg knew what
he wanted, and he sure didn't want much of what I'd written. When I finally got that through my thick skull, I
skulked away into the night, never to hear from "Phil"
again—until he sent me one free ticket for opening night a
year and a half later.

Phil and his gang went on to use my story as the basis for

the wildly successful (and depressing) play, *The Voice of Our Shadow*. Among other things, it is about sadness and the small dreams of the young, and besides running for two years on Broadway, where it won the Pulitzer Prize, it was made into a halfway-decent film. I retained a small but lucrative percentage of those subsidiary and world rights, thank God.

The hoopla over the play began in my senior year in college. I thought it was great at the beginning and horrible from then on. People were convinced I had written the whole thing, and I spent most of the time explaining that my contribution had been little more than, well, microscopic. On opening night, I sat in the audience and stared at the young actors playing Ross and Bobby and those other guys and girls I had known so well a hundred years ago in my life. I watched them being changed and distorted, and when I walked out of the theater I ached with guilt at the death of my brother. But did I ache to tell anyone what had actually happened that day? No. Guilt can be molded. It is a funny kind of clay; if you know how to handle it right, you can twist and knead and form or place it anyway you want. I know that is a generalization, but it is what I did; and as I got older, I had less and less trouble rationalizing the fact that I had murdered my brother. It was an accident. I had never meant for it to happen. He was a monster and had deserved it. If *he* hadn't brought up the subject of masturbation that day . . . It all helped me to punch the bare, ghastly fact that I had done it into the shape I wanted.

Within a few months I had more money than King Tut. I was also exhausted and embittered by the same well-meant questions and the same disappointed looks on faces when I told them no, no, I didn't write the *play*, you see . . .

When I discovered that my university offered a six-week course in modern German literature in Vienna, I jumped at

the chance. I had majored in German because it was hard
and challenging and something I wanted to become very
good at in my life. I was convinced I would be able to surface again all clean and absolved after a few months of
sacher torte, outings on the Blue Danube, and Robert
Musil. I arranged it so my six weeks there would come at the
end of the school year, which would allow me to stay
through the summer if I liked the town.

I loved Vienna from the beginning. The Viennese are
well fed, obedient, and a little behind the times in almost
everything they do. Because of this, or because the city is exotic in that it is far to the East—the last free, decadent
stronghold before you roll over the flat gray plains into
Hungary or Czechoslovakia—all my memories of it are
washed in a slow, end-of-the-afternoon light. Sometimes
even now, even after everything that has happened, I wish
very much that I was back there.

There are cafés where you can sit all morning over one
cup of wonderful coffee and read a book without anyone
ever disturbing you. Small, smelly movie theaters with
wooden seats, where a couple of sad-looking models put on a
"live" fashion show for you before the feature goes on. I had
a favorite *gasthaus* where the waiter brought dogs water in a
white porcelain bowl with the name of the restaurant on the
side.

It is also the only city I know that gives up its best parts
grudgingly, unhappily. Paris slaps you in the face with oce-
anic boulevards, golden croissants, and charm on every
square inch of its surface. New York sneers—completely assured and indifferent. It knows that no matter how much
dirt or crime or fear there is, it is still the center of everything. It can do what it wants because it knows you will always need it.

Most visitors like Vienna at first sight (including myself!)
because of the Opera or the Ringstrasse or the Brueghels in
the Kunsthistorisches Museum, but these things are only

grand camouflage. The first summer I was there, I discovered that beneath the lovely gloss is a sad, suspicious city that reached its peak a hundred, two hundred years ago. It is now regarded by the world as a delightful oddity—a Miss Havisham in her wedding dress—and the Viennese know it.

Everything went right for me. I met a nice girl from the Tirol, and we had a fling that left us tired but unscarred. She was a tour guide for one of the companies in town and consequently knew every nook and cranny in the place: the Jugendstil swimming pool at the top of the Wienerwald, a cozy restaurant where they served the original Czech Budweiser beer, a walk through the First District that made you feel as if you were back in the fifteenth century. We had a rainy weekend in Venice and a sunny one in Salzburg. She took me to the airport at the end of August, and we promised to write. A few months later she did, telling me she was marrying a nice computer salesman from Charlottesville, Virginia, and if I was ever down their way . . .

My father picked me up at the airport and, as soon as we were in the car, told me Mother had leukemia. What came to mind was a picture of the last time I had seen her: a white hospital room—white curtains, bedspread, chairs. In the middle of the bed hovering over that eternity of white was her small red head. Her hair had been chopped short, and she no longer made the quick, sharp movements of a hummingbird. Because they kept her sedated most of the time, it often took minutes before she fully recognized anyone.

"Mama? It's Joe. I'm here, Mama. *Joe.*"

"Joe? Joe. Joe! Joe and Ross! Where are my two boys?" She wasn't disappointed when we told her Ross wasn't there. She accepted it as she accepted each spoonful of colorless soup or creamed spinach from her plate.

I went directly to the hospital. The only obvious change was a pronounced thinness about her face. Taken together, her features and the wrong color of her skin reminded me of a very thin, very old letter written on gray paper in violet ink. She asked me where I had been; when I said Europe, she gazed for a time at the wall as if she was trying to figure out what Europe was. She was dead by Christmas.

After her funeral my father and I took a week off and flew down to the heat, colors, and freshness of the Virgin Islands. We sat on the beach, swam, and took long, panting walks up into the hills. Each night the beauty of the sunset made us feel sad, empty, and heroic. We agreed on that. We drank dark rum and talked until two or three in the morning. I told him I wanted to go back and live in Europe after I had graduated. Two more of my short stories had been published, and I wondered excitedly if I might have the makings of a real writer. I realize now he would have liked me to stay with him for a while, but he said he thought Europe was a good idea.

My last semester in college was full of a girl named Olivia Lofting. It was the first time I'd ever really fallen hard for someone, and there was a period when I needed Olivia as I needed air. She liked me because I had money and a certain prestige on campus, but she kept reminding me her heart belonged to a guy who had graduated the year before and was serving a hitch in the Army. I did what I could to lure her away, but she remained true to him despite the fact we'd been sleeping together since our third date.

May came, and so did Olivia's boyfriend, home on leave. I saw the two of them one afternoon at the Student Center. They were so obviously mad for each other and so obviously tired from making love that I went right to the bathroom and sat on a toilet for an hour with my face in my hands.

She called after he left, but I didn't have the strength to see her again. Oddly enough, my refusal sparked her interest, and for the few weeks left of the year, we had one endless conversation after another over the phone. The last time we talked she demanded we get together. I asked if she was a sadist, and with a delighted laugh she said she probably was. I had barely enough willpower to say no, but did I ever hate myself after I hung up and realized how unnecessarily empty my bed would be that night.

Although Vienna was always in the back of my mind, I flew to London and spent the summer trying on different cities—Munich, Copenhagen, Milan—before I realized there really was only one place for me.

Ironically, I arrived just as the German version of *The Voice of Our Shadow* was premiering at the Theatre an der Josefstädt. Out of what I'm sure he thought was kindness, Phil Westberg told the Austrians I was there, and for a month or two I was the belle of the ball. Again, all I did was backpedal about my involvement in the original production, only this time *auf deutsch.*

Luckily the Viennese critics didn't like the play; after a month's run it packed its bag and went back to America. That ended my notoriety as well, and from then on I was blissfully anonymous. The one good thing that came from *Shadow* rearing its confusing head in Wien was that I met a lot of important people who, again assuming I'd been the moving force behind the play, began to give me writing assignments as soon as they heard I wanted to settle down there. The pay for these assignments was usually terrible, but I was making new contacts all the time. When the *International Herald Tribune* did a supplement on Austria, a friend snuck me in the back door, and they published a little article I'd done on the Bregenz Summer Festival.

About the time I started making money from my articles, my father remarried and I returned to America for the wedding. It was my first time back in two years, and I was bowled over by the speed and intensity of the States. So much stimulus! So many things to see and buy and do! I loved it for two weeks, but then hurried back to my Vienna, where things were just the way I liked them—quiet and settled and cozily dull.

I was twenty-four, and in some distant, mute part of my brain I had the notion it was time to try writing my world-beater, gargantuan novel. When I returned from America I started . . . and started again and started again . . . until I had worn out all my thin beginnings. That was all right, but too quickly I realized I had no middles or ends to work on instead. At that point I bowed out of the race for the Great American Novel.

I am convinced every writer would like to be either a poet or a novelist, but in my case the realization that I would never be another Hart Crane or Tolstoy wasn't too painful. It might have been a couple of years earlier, but I was being regularly published now, and there were even a few people around who knew who I was. Not many, but some.

After living a couple of years in Vienna, what I missed most was having a good close friend. For a while I thought I'd found one in a sleek, classy French woman who worked as a translator for the United Nations. We hit it off from the first and for a few weeks were inseparable. Then we went to bed, and the familiarity that had come so easily was pushed aside by the purple mysteries of sex. We were lovers for a time, but it was easy to see we were better as friends than as lovers. Unfortunately too, because there was no way back once we had turned the lights down low. She transferred to Geneva, and I went back to being prolific . . . and lonely.

PART TWO

|

India and Paul Tate were movie crazy, and we originally met at one of the few theaters in town that showed films in English. Hitchcock's *Strangers on a Train* was being revived, and I had done quite a bit of homework preparing for it. I had read Patricia Highsmith's Thomas Ripley books before I tackled the novel on which the movie was based. Then I read MacShane's biography of Raymond Chandler with the long section in it on the making of the classic.

In fact, I was finishing the biography while I sat in the theater lobby waiting for the show to begin. Some people sat down next to me. In a few seconds I realized they were speaking English.

"Come on, Paul, don't be a dodo. It's Raymond Chandler."

"Nunnally Johnson."

"Paul—"

"India, who was right about the Lubitsch film? Huh?"

"Stop dangling that dumb movie in my face. So what if you were right once in your life? P.S., who was right *yester-*

day about Fielder Cook directing *A Big Hand for the Little Lady?*"

Normally that kind of argument between a couple is tacky and loud, but the tone of their voices assured you they were not really arguing; no lurking anger or bared fangs anywhere.

"Excuse me? Uh, do you speak English?"

I turned and nodded and saw India Tate for the first time. It was summer; she had on a lemon-yellow T-shirt and new dark blue jeans. Her smile was a challenge.

I nodded, inwardly delighted to be talking to such an attractive woman.

"Great. Do you know who wrote this movie? I don't mean the book, I mean the screenplay. I'm having a fight with my husband here about it." She shot her thumb in his direction as if she were hitchhiking.

"Well, I've just read a whole chapter on it in this book. It says Chandler wrote it and Hitchcock directed, but then they ended up hating each other when it was done." I tried to phrase it so both of them would feel that they had won the argument.

It didn't work. She turned to her husband and stuck her tongue out at him for a split second. He smiled and, reaching over her lap, offered me his hand. "You don't have to pay any attention to her. I'm Paul Tate, and the tongue here is my wife, India." He shook hands the way you should—strong and very much there.

"How do you do? I'm Joseph Lennox."

"You see, Paul? I knew I was right! I knew you were Joseph Lennox. I remember seeing your picture in *Wiener* magazine. That's why I made us sit here."

"Recognized for the first time in my life!"

I fell in love with her on the spot. I was already halfway gone once I'd seen her face and that wonderful yellow T-shirt, but then her knowing who I was . . .

"Joseph Lennox. God, we saw *The Voice of Our Shadow* two times on Broadway and then once up in Massachusetts in summer stock. Paul even bought the O. Henry collection with 'Wooden Pajamas' in it."

Nervous now and unhappy that the recognition was due to the play, I fumbled with the Chandler biography and dropped it on the floor. India and I simultaneously bent over to pick it up, and I caught a faint scent of lemon and some kind of good sweet soap.

The usher walked by and said we could go in. Getting up, we made quick plans to go out for coffee afterward. Right away I noticed they moved ahead of me and sat in the first row. Who would want to sit there? Very little of the movie made sense to me because I spent most of my time either looking at the backs of their heads or wondering who these interesting people were.

"Are summers here always this humid, Joe? It feels as if a big dog is breathing on me. I wish we were back at my mother's apartment in New York."

"India, every time we're there in the summer you complain about the heat."

"Sure, Paul, but at least that's *New York* heat. There's a big difference."

She said no more. He looked at me and rolled his eyes. We were sitting at an outside table in front of the Café Landtmann. A red and white tram clacked by, and the colored fountains across the street in Rathaus Park shot their streams up through the thick night.

"It does get pretty hot here now. That's why all the Viennese go to their country houses in August."

She looked at me and shook her head. "It's nuts. Look, I don't know anything about this place yet, but isn't tourism supposed to be Austria's main source of income? Most tourists travel in August, right? So they get to Vienna and the whole joint is closed up for vacation. Tighter than anything in Italy or France, huh, Paul?"

We had been there half an hour. Already I'd noticed India did most of the talking, unless she egged Paul on to tell a particular anecdote or story. But they both listened carefully when the other spoke. I felt a hollow rush of jealousy when I noticed their complete mutual interest.

Some time later I asked Paul, who turned out to be a delightfully garrulous person away from his wife, why he clammed up when he was around her.

"I guess because she's so wonderfully strange, Joe. Don't you think? I mean, we've been married for years, and yet she still amazes me with all of the weird things she says! Usually I can't wait to hear what's going to come next. It's always been like that."

When there was a lull in the conversation that first night and everything was quiet, I asked how they had met.

"You tell him, Paul. I want to watch this tram go by."

We all watched it go by. After a few seconds, Paul sat forward and put his big hands on his knees.

"When I was in the Navy I went out and bought this screwy Hawaiian shirt when my ship docked in Honolulu. It was the most hideous piece of clothing that ever existed. Yellow with blue coconut trees and green monkeys."

"You stop lying, Paul! You loved every scrawny little palm tree on that shirt and you know it. I thought you were going to cry when it fell apart." She reached across the table and brushed her fingertips over his cheek. I looked away, embarrassed and jealous of her casual tenderness.

"Yes, I guess I did, but it's hard to admit it now."

"Yeah? Well, shut up, because you looked great in it! He really did, Joe. He was standing on this street corner in the middle of San Francisco waiting for a trolley. He looked like an ad for Bacardi rum. I walked up to him and told him he was the only guy I'd ever seen who actually looked good in one of those goony shirts."

"You didn't say I looked good, India—you said I looked *too* good. You made it sound as if I was one of those creeps who read science fiction novels and carry five million keys on their belt loop."

"Oh, sure, but I said that later—after we went out for the drink."

Paul turned to me and nodded. "That's right. The first thing she said was I looked good. We stood on the corner for a while and talked about Hawaii. She'd never been there and wanted to know if *poi* really tasted like wallpaper paste. I ended up asking her if she'd like to go someplace for a drink. She said yes and that was that. Bingo."

"What do you mean, 'that was that'? 'That was that,' except for the fact I didn't see you again for two years. 'Bingo,' my foot!"

Paul shrugged at her correction. It was unimportant to him. No one said anything, and the only sounds were cars passing on the Ringstrasse.

"See, Joe, I gave him my address and telephone number, right? But he never called, the rat. Ah, what did I care? I just wrote him off as some little twit in his ugly Hawaiian shirt and didn't think about him again until he called me two years later when I was living in Los Angeles."

"Two *years*? How come you waited two years, Paul?" I wouldn't have waited two seconds to claim India Tate.

"Hmm. I thought she was okay and all, but nothing to go nuts about."

"Thanks, mac!"

"You're welcome. I was still in the Navy and my boat put into San Francisco for Thanksgiving. We were given a couple of days' liberty. I thought it would be fun to call her up. She wasn't living in her old digs anymore, but I was able to trace her through a roommate to Los Angeles."

41

If it's possible, India was glaring and smiling at him at the same time. "Yeah, I was working at Walt Disney Studios. Doing fascinating things like drawing Mickey Mouse's ears. Neat, huh? I was bored, so when he called and asked if I would come up and spend the holiday with him, I said yes. Even if he was a twit in Hawaiian shirts. We ended up having a good time, and before he left he asked me to marry him."

"Just like that?"

They nodded together. "Yup, and I said yes just like that. You think I wanted to draw Scrooge McDuck for the rest of my life? He shipped out, and I didn't see him this time for two months. When I did we got married."

"You and Scrooge McDuck?"

"No, me and twit." She hitchhiked her thumb his way again. "We did it in New York."

"New York?"

"Right. In Manhattan. We got married and had dinner at the Four Seasons and then went to a movie."

"*Dr. No,*" Paul piped up.

We had ordered more coffee despite the waiter's having made it clear to us by his curtness that it was closing time and he wanted us out.

"So, what are *you* working on now, Joe?"

"Oh, I've been poking around this one idea I've had for a while. It would be a kind of oral history of Vienna in World War II. So much has already been written about the battles and all that, but what interests me is recording the stories of the other people who were involved—especially the women, and others who were kids then. Can you imagine living through years of that? Their stories are just as incredible as the ones of the guys who fought. Really, you'd be knocked out if you heard what some of them went through."

I was getting excited because the project interested me and because I had told only a few people about it. Until that moment it had been one of those "gotta do that someday" dreams that never get done.

"Let me give you an example. There is a woman I know who worked for an insane asylum out in the Nineteenth District. The Nazis ordered her bosses to get the whole bunch of cuckoos out of there. This woman ended up carting them out of the city and up to an old *Schloss* on the Czech border, and amazingly they survived until the end of the war. It was straight out of that film *King of Hearts.*"

India shifted in her chair and rubbed her slim bare arms. The night had grown suddenly cooler and it was getting late.

"Joe, do you mind if I ask you something?"

Thinking it would be about the new book, I was completely taken off guard by her question when it came.

"What did you think of *The Voice of Our Shadow?* Did you like it? The whole play is so different from your short story, isn't it?"

"Yes, you're right. And to tell you the deep, deep truth, I've never liked the play, even when I saw it with the original cast in New York. I know that's biting the hand that fed me, but everything was distorted so much. It's a good play, but it isn't my story, if you see what I mean."

"Did you grow up with guys like that? Were you a tough guy?"

"No. I was Charlie the Chicken. I didn't even know what a gang was until someone told me. No, my brother was tough and his best friend was a real juvenile delinquent, but I was the kind who hid under the bed most of the time when the going got tough."

"You're kidding."

"Absolutely not. I hated to fight, I hated to smoke, I hated to get drunk . . . blood made me gag . . ."

They were smiling, and I smiled with them. India took out a cigarette—unfiltered, I noticed—and Paul lit it for her.

"What is your brother like? Is he still a tough guy or does he sell insurance or something?"

"Well, you see, my brother is dead."

"Ooops, sorry about that." She dipped her shoulders and looked away.

"It's okay. He died when I was thirteen."

"Thirteen? Really? How old was he?"

"Sixteen. He was electrocuted."

"Electrocuted? How did that happen?"

"He fell on a third rail."

"God!"

"Yes. I was there. Uh, waiter, could we have the check?"

2

Paul turned out to be kind and witty and scatterbrained. He could listen to the most boring person talk for hours and still look as if he was fascinated. When the person left, he would usually say something funny or nasty about them, but if they happened to come back later, he would be the same open, thoughtful listener and confidant.

He was from the Midwest and had a friendly, slightly bewildered face that was prematurely jowly and made you think he was much older than his wife. The Tates were, however, exactly the same age.

He worked for one of the large international agencies in Vienna. He would never be specific about his job, but it had something to do with trade fairs in Communist countries. I often wondered if he was a spy, as are so many other "businessmen" in that town. Once, when I pressed him on it, he told me even the Czechs, Poles, and Rumanians had things they wanted to sell to the outside world, and that these fairs were where they got a chance to "strut their stuff."

India Tate resembled a character you see in 1930s or '40s movies played by either Joan Blondell or Ida Lupino: a pretty face, but a hard, tight pretty. On the surface she's a tough, no-nonsense gal, but one who becomes increasingly vulnerable the longer you know her. Like Paul, she was in her early forties, but it didn't show on either of their figures because they were manic about exercising and keeping fit. They once showed me the yoga they did together every morning for an hour. I tried some of it, but couldn't even lift myself off the ground. I knew they didn't like that, and a few days later Paul quietly suggested I start some kind of program that would put me back in shape. I did it for a while but quit when it started to bore me.

On learning they were being transferred to Vienna from London, India decided to take a year off from teaching and learn German. According to Paul, she was naturally adept at languages, and a month or two after her classes at the University of Vienna began, he told me, she was able to translate the German news on the radio for him. I didn't know how much of this was true because she refused to speak anything but English whenever the three of us went out together. Once, when absolutely pressed, she stuttered out a slow, frightened question to a train conductor. It sounded grammatically correct, but it also had a strong Oklahoma accent tied around it like a bow.

"India, how come you never speak German?"

"Because I sound like Andy Devine when I talk."

She was like that in so many ways. It was easy to see how talented and intelligent she was, and that there were a number of things she could have sculpted a life out of. But she was a perfectionist and avoided or played down almost anything she did that came out only "half good" as far as she was concerned.

For instance, there were her drawings. Besides the German course, she had decided that during her "free" year she would do something she had had in mind to do for years —she was going to illustrate her childhood. When they were living in London she had taught art at one of the international schools there. During her free periods she'd made over a hundred preliminary sketches, but getting her to show them to me was impossible at first. When she finally did, I was so impressed I didn't know what to say.

The Shadow was one of those humpbacked Art Deco radios with cozy round black dials and the names of a million exotic places on them that were supposedly at your beck and call. This radio was on a table set far back in the room toward the top of the drawing. Jutting out stiff and doll-like from the bottom were three pairs of legs set right next to one another—a man's, a child's (black patent-leather shoes and short white socks), and a woman's (bare with pointed, high-heel shoes). Nothing more of these people could be seen, but the most wonderful, eerie part of the work was that all three sets of legs were pointing toward the radio, giving you the impression the bottoms of their feet were watching the radio like a television set. I told that to India and she laughed. She said she had never thought of it that way before, but it made sense. In all her work, that one-quarter naïve, one-quarter eerie quality came through again and again.

In another one, an empty gray room was totally bare except for a pillow in flight across the middle of the picture. The hand that had thrown it was there in the corner, but in its frozen openness it had lost all human qualities and was suddenly, disturbingly something else. She said she planned on calling the final version *Pillow Fight.*

Only one of her pictures was on actual display in their apartment. It was entitled *Little Boy.* It was a still life, painted in fragile, washed-out watercolors. On an oak table were a shiny black top hat (the type the Germans call a *Zylinder*) and a pair of spotless white gloves. That was all: tan wooden table, black hat, white gloves. *Little Boy.*

The first time I went to their home I stared at it for a while and then politely asked what the title meant. They looked at each other and then, as if on cue, laughed at the same time.

"That one's not from my childhood, Joe. Paul has this crazy thing he does sometimes—"

"Shh, India, don't say a word! Maybe we ll introduce the two of them sometime, huh?"

Her face lit up like a candle. She loved the idea. She laughed and laughed, but neither of them made any attempt to clue me in. Later she said she had painted the picture for Paul as an anniversary present. I had noticed there was an inscription in the lower-left-hand corner: *To Mister from Missus—Promises to Keep.*

They had lucked into a great big apartment in the Ninth District not far from the Danube Canal. But they spent little time there. Both of them said they felt compelled to be out and on the move as much as possible. Consequently, they were almost never home when I called.

"I don't understand why the two of you are always out. Your apartment is so nice and warm."

India shot Paul an intimate, secret smile that fled as soon as she looked back at me. "I guess we're afraid there will be something out there we'll miss if we stay home."

We met the first week in July, when they had been in town for over a month. They had seen the usual sights, but now I eagerly appointed myself their special guide and gave them every bit of Vienna I had accumulated (and hoarded) in the years I had lived there.

Those dreamy, warm days passed in a delightful blur. I would finish my writing as early as I could and then two or three times a week would meet them somewhere for lunch. Paul was on vacation until the end of July, so we moved slowly and sensually through those days as if they were a great meal we never wanted to finish. At least that's how I felt, and I could sometimes sense their happiness was growing too.

I began to feel as if I had been fueled with some fabulous high-octane gasoline. I wrote and did research like a mad machine in the morning, played with the Tates in the afternoon, and went home to bed at night feeling that my life couldn't possibly be much fuller than it was right at that moment. I had found the friends I'd been looking for all along.

On my twenty-fifth birthday, they put the cherry on top of the cake.

I was sitting at my desk on August 19, working on an interview I was doing on spec for a Swiss magazine. It was my birthday, and because birthdays almost always depressed the hell out of me, I was trying hard to work my way through this one with as few distractions as possible. I had had an early dinner at a neighborhood *gasthaus*, and instead of going to a café and reading for an hour, as I usually did, I raced home and restlessly pushed the sheets of typescript around my desk in a vain attempt to forget that no one in the world had tipped me a nod on my Day of Days.

When the doorbell rang, I was frowning at the minuscule pile of pages I had done. I was wearing an old sweatshirt and a pair of blue jeans.

An old man in a seedy but still-elegant chauffeur's outfit was standing there with his cap in his hand. He wore black leather gloves that looked very expensive. He looked me over as if I were last week's lettuce and said in a nice *hoch-*

deutsch accent that "the car" was downstairs and the lady and gentleman were waiting. Was I ready?

I smiled and asked what he was talking about.

"You *are* Mr. Lennox?"

"Yes."

"Then I have been told to come for you, sir."

"Who, uh, who sent you?"

"The lady and gentleman in the car, sir. I assume they hired the limousine."

"Limousine?" I squinted suspiciously and pushed him a little to one side so I could peek out the door into the hall. Paul liked to play tricks, and I was dubious of anything he had his finger in. No one was out there. "They're down in the car?"

"Yes, sir." He sighed and pulled one of the gloves farther up onto his hand.

I asked him to describe them, and he described Paul and India Tate in evening clothes.

"Evening? You mean formal? A tuxedo?"

"Yes, sir."

"Oh, God! Look, uh, look, you tell them I'll be down in ten minutes. Ten minutes, okay?"

"Yes, sir, ten minutes." He gave me one last tired look and marched off.

No shower. Rip the tuxedo off the hanger way in the back of the closet. I hadn't worn it in months, and it was full of creases. So what? Seconds of trouble buttoning the silk buttons with shaky, happy hands. What were those two up to? How great! Fabulous! They had *known* it was my birthday. They had even double-checked the date a few days before. Why had they hired a limousine? I took a fat glug of mouthwash and spat it loudly in the sink as I was turning out the light and heading for the door. At the last second I remembered to take my keys.

A silver Mercedes-Benz 450 was purring majestically in front of my apartment house. Inside I could see the chauffeur (with his cap on now—all business) lit by the calm yellow of the dashboard lights. I stepped over to look in the back seat and there they were, champagne glasses in hand, the bottle sticking out of a silver bucket on the darkly carpeted floor.

The window on my side zizzed down, and India's wonderful face peeped out of that rich inner gloom.

"What's up, Birthday Boy? Wanna go for a ride?"

"Hi! What are you doing here? What's with this silver chariot?"

"Joe Lennox, for once in your measly little life, don't ask any questions and get in the damned car!" Paul's voice rumbled out.

When I got in, India slid over so I could sit between them. Paul handed me a chilled glass of champagne and gave my knee a short, friendly squeeze.

"Happy birthday, Joey! Have we got some big plans for *you* tonight!"

"And how!" India clinked her glass to mine and kissed my cheek.

"Like what?"

"Like sit back and you'll see. You wanna spoil the surprise?"

India told the driver to go to the first place on their list.

The champagne lasted until the end of the ride, which turned out to be Schloss Greifenstein, a huge and wonderfully forbidding castle about half an hour out of Vienna. It is perched high on a hill overlooking a bend in the Danube. There's a splendid restaurant up there, and that's where we had my birthday dinner. When it was over, I really had to work hard to keep from crying. What special people. I had never had a surprise like that in my whole life.

"This . . . this is some night for me."

"Joey, you're our *boy*. Do you know how much you helped us when we first got here? There's no way in the world we'd let you get away without a party tonight!"

India took my hand and held it. "Now, don't get all worked up about it. We've been planning to do it forever. Paul thought up the idea of coming here for dinner, but that's nothing. Wait till you see what I—"

"Pipe down, India, don't *tell* him! We'll just go."

They were already standing, and I hadn't even seen anyone pay the bill.

"What's going on? You mean there's more?"

"Damned right, buddy. This here's just the first course. Let's go—our big silver bullet's waiting."

More turned out to be three chocolate sundaes at McDonald's on Mariahilferstrasse, with the Mercedes waiting for us outside. India bought the driver a sundae, too. That was followed by a long coffee at the Café Museum across from the Opera, and then adjoining rooms for the night at the Imperial Hotel on the Ringstrasse. If you haven't been to Vienna, the Imperial is the place where the likes of Henry Kissinger stay when they're in town for a conference. The price of rooms begins at a hundred and forty dollars.

When we were properly installed (and the bellboy had given us all an angry, insulted look because we had no baggage), and we'd bounced on each of the beds, Paul opened the door and paraded into my room with a Monopoly game he said he'd bought fresh for the occasion. We finished the night playing Monopoly on the floor and eating a terrific sacher torte ordered from room service. At four in the morning Paul said he had to go to work that day and had to get at least a little sleep.

We were all ruffled, frazzled, and giddy as hell from no sleep, being silly, and laughter. I hugged the two of them when they went off to bed with a force I hoped told them how much the night and their friendship meant to me.

3

"What was your brother like? Like you?"

India and I were sitting on a bench in the Stadtpark, waiting for Paul to join us. The leaves had just begun to turn color, and the sharp, smoky smell of real autumn was in the air.

"No, we were incredibly different."

"In what way?" She had a brown paper cone of warm chestnuts in her lap, and she peeled the shell off each with the utmost care. I liked watching her do it. The chestnut surgeon.

"He was clever and cagey and sneaky. He would have made the world's greatest diplomat if he hadn't had such a bad temper." A pigeon walked over and snatched up a cigarette butt at our feet.

"How did you feel about him after he died?"

I wondered if I would ever be close enough to her to tell the real story. I wondered if I wanted to tell anyone the real story. What would it accomplish? Would it truly make things better? Would I feel less guilty after I'd given someone else the truth to hold with me? I looked hard at India and decided to test some of that truth on her.

"Do you want to know something? I felt worse when my mother was committed to the insane asylum. My brother, Ross, was *bad*, India. By the time he died he'd done so many mean things to me I felt like a punching bag. Sometimes I don't think he cared if he was my brother or not. He was that cruel, or sadistic, or whatever you want to call it. So in my heart of hearts I was glad I wasn't going to get hit anymore."

"What's so bad about that? It sounds right." She offered me a fat chestnut.

"What do you mean?"

"I mean just what I said—it sounds right. Joe, kids are little shits, I don't care what anyone says about how cute and sweet they are. They're greedy and egotistical and don't understand anything outside their own needs. You didn't feel bad when your brother died because he wasn't going to hit you anymore. It makes total sense. What's the problem? Were you a masochist?"

"No, but it also makes me sound terrible." I was half indignant.

"Hey, don't get me wrong—you *were* terrible. We were all terrible when we were little. Did you ever see how vicious and monstrous kids are to one another? And I'm not just talking about in the sandbox either, where they bang each other over the head with their trucks! Teenagers . . . God, teach them for a while if you want to learn about mean. There is nothing in the world as small and malicious and self-centered as a fifteen-year-old. No, Joey, don't crucify yourself over it. People don't become human until they're around twenty-two years old, and then they're just beginning. Don't laugh, I'm completely serious."

"Okay, but I'm only twenty-five!"

"Who said you were human?" She ate the last chestnut and threw the shell at me.

An editor who was interested in my idea for the war book was coming over to the Frankfurt Book Fair and asked if I'd come up so we could talk about it. I readily agreed because it gave me a good excuse to take a train ride (which I love) and to meet some New York book people. I mentioned the trip to Paul only because the subject of train travel came up in conversation one day when we were having lunch together. We went on to reminisce about the great train trips we'd taken on the *Super Chief,* the *Transalpin,* the *Blue Train* from Paris to the Riviera . . .

This was at the beginning of October, when the Tates were busy going to a month-long adventure-film festival at the Albertina museum in town. The night I left, I knew they were due to see a double feature they'd been talking about for weeks—*North by Northwest* and *The Thirty-nine Steps*. We had coffee together at the Landtmann in the late afternoon and said we would rendezvous somewhere as soon as I got back to town. Fine, see you then. When we separated, I stopped, turned, and watched them walk away. India was talking excitedly to Paul, as if she'd just met him after a long separation and had many new things to tell him. I smiled and thought of how quickly our relationship had blossomed. I smiled even more when I thought how great it was to have both Vienna and them to return to.

I've never been lonely in either an airport or a train station. The sounds and smells of travelers, dust, and huge metal; people rushing around in every direction; arrivals, departures, and expectations in their veins instead of blood. If I am ever traveling somewhere, I try to be in the station at least an hour before departure so I can sit somewhere and enjoy the bustle. You can always go to a train station and sit there and enjoy it, but it's better if you're on your way someplace or expecting someone.

The original Vienna Westbahnhof was destroyed in the war, and the building that replaced it is one of those modern boxy things with no character at all. What saves it in the end is that about eighty percent of the place is glass—windows everywhere—and no matter where you are, you have a panoramic view of that part of the city. It's wonderful to go in the afternoon and watch the sun drift through the windows and over everything. At night, climb the wide middle staircase, and once at the top, turn around quickly: the Café Westend across the street is full and bright, trams stream by in every direction, and the neon ads on the sides of the buildings splatter the dark with words and catch phrases that remind you that you're in a far country. Car insurance is *Interunfall Versicherung,* cars are Puch and Lada, Mercedes. Coca-Cola as well, only here *Coke macht mehr draus!*

I had a cup of coffee at one of the stand-up buffets and then started the long hike down the endless platform to the car with my reserved couchette. The lights in the train were off when I passed through the departure gate, but they suddenly clicked on all at once; street lamps at the end of dusk. A workman and a baggage porter, both dressed in different shades of blue, were leaning against a metal support post, talking and smoking. Since we were the only ones there, long appraising looks passed back and forth. This was their land until train time—what was I doing out there so early, trespassing? The porter looked at his watch, scowled, and flicked his cigarette away. The two of them separated without another word, and the workman walked over to the other side of the platform and climbed into a darkened first-class coach that said on a white and black sign that sometime deep in the night it would be going to Ostend, and then on to London.

Far up the tracks a single black engine scooted shrilly away and out of sight. I hefted my overnight bag and kept looking at the numbers on the sides of the cars. I wanted to be in my compartment. I wanted to be in my seat, eating the jumbo hero sandwich I'd made at home for dinner and watching the other people arrive.

The light was out in one compartment of my car. Climbing up the steep metal stairs, I made a silent bet with myself that it would be the light in mine. It would be broken, and if I wanted to do any reading before I went to sleep, I would have to walk ten cars back to find an empty seat. The light in the corridor was on, but sure enough, the dark one had my berth number on the door. The blue curtains were drawn across both windows. The Inner Sanctum. I reached down and pulled the door handle, but it didn't move. I put my bag down and pulled with both hands. Nothing happened. I looked up and down the corridor for anyone who could help, but it was empty. Cursing, I snatched at the damned thing again and pulled with all my might. Not an inch. I gave the door a kick.

Immediately the curtains began to slide aside. I took a startled step backward. A theme from *Scheherezade* came on faintly. A match flared and broke the inner dark. It moved slowly left and right, then stopped. It went out, and a dull yellow flashlight beam came on in its place.

Outside, I heard the *chunk* of railroad cars being coupled together. The lemony light held, motionless; then it moved over a white-gloved hand that held a black top hat. A second white hand joined it on the other side of the shiny brim, and for a moment the hat moved in time to the sultry music.

"Surprise!" The light blasted on, and India Tate stood with a bottle of champagne in her hand. Behind her, Paul had the top hat on his head at a rakish slant and was opening another bottle with his clown-white gloves. I remembered the painting on the wall of their apartment. So this was Little Boy.

"Jesus Christ, you guys!"

The door slid open, and she yanked me into the little hot room.

"Where're the cups, Paul?"

"What are you doing here? What happened to your movies?"

"Be quiet and take a glass of this. Don't you want any of your going-away champagne?"

I did, and she slopped so much into my cup that it foamed up and over the edge and onto the dirty floor.

"I hope you like this stuff, Joey. I think it's Albanian." Paul still had his gloves on when he held his cup out to be filled.

"But what's going on? Aren't you missing *North by Northwest?*"

"Yup, but we decided you deserved a proper send-off. So

drink up and don't say anything else about it. Believe it or not, Lennox, we love you more than Cary Grant."

"Baloney."

"You're absolutely right—*almost* as much as Cary Grant. I would now like to propose a toast to the three of us. Comrades in arms." A man walked past in the narrow corridor behind me. I heard his footsteps. India held her cup up to him and said, *"Prosit,* pardner!" He kept walking. "Anyway, to get back to what I was saying, I would like to propose that we all drink to a truly wonderful life."

Paul echoed her words and nodded in total agreement. They turned to me and held their Dixie cups up to be toasted. I was afraid my heart would break.

Sometimes the mail in Austria is very slow; it can take three days for a letter to get from one side of Vienna to the other. I wasn't surprised when I received a Tate postcard from the town of Drosendorf in the Waldviertel section of the country a week after I'd returned from Frankfurt. That night on the train during our party they'd said they were going up there for a few days of rest and relaxation.

The card was written in India's extremely neat, almost too-tight, up-and-down script. Every time I saw it I was reminded of the sample of Frederick Rolfe's handwriting in A. J. A. Symons's fascinating biography, *The Quest for Corvo.* Rolfe, who called himself Baron Corvo and wrote *Hadrian VII,* was nutty as a fruitcake. As soon as I knew her well enough to be able to kid her, I'd made a point of pressing the book on India and instantly turning to the page to show her the amazingly similar scrawl. She was not thrilled by the comparison, although Paul said I had her dead to rights.

Dear Joey.
There is a big church here in the center of town. The big attraction inside the big church is a skeleton of a

woman all dolled up in a wedding gown, I think.
She's behind glass and has a bouquet of dead flowers
on her.

Little hugs,
Mr. & Mrs. Little Boy

The postcard was interesting only because neither of them liked to talk about anything that had to do with death. Several weeks before, a man in Paul's office had keeled over dead at his desk from a cerebral hemorrhage. Apparently Paul was so shaken by it that he had to leave work for the day. He said he'd gone for a walk in the park, but his legs were shaking so much that after a few minutes he had to sit down.

Once, when I asked him if he ever saw himself growing old and dying, he said no. Instead, he said, he envisioned an old man with gray hair and wrinkles who was called Paul Tate but wasn't him.

"What do you mean? There'll be another you in your body?"

"Yes, don't look at me as if I'm goony. It's like working a shift in a factory, see? I'm working one of the middle ones—the thirty-five to forty-five shift, get it? Then some other man checks into my body and takes it from there. He'll know all about being old and arthritic and that sort of thing, so it won't bother him."

"He's got the old-age shift, huh?"

"Exactly! He comes in for the midnight-to-seven spot. It makes good sense, Joey, so don't laugh like that. Do you realize how many different beings you are in a lifetime? How all your hopes and opinions, everything, change every six or seven years? Aren't all the cells in our bodies supposed to be different every few years? It's just the same. Listen, there was a time when all India and I wanted was a saltbox house on the coast of Maine with lots of land around us. We wanted to raise dogs, can you believe it? Now just the thought of that kind of permanence makes me start to itch. Who's to say the little guys in our bodies who wanted to live in the house haven't been replaced by a whole new bunch who like to travel around and see new things? Apply that to who we are at the different times in our lives: You've got one crew that takes you from one to seven. Then they're replaced by the group that steers you through puberty and that whole mess. Joe, are you going to tell me you're the same Joe Lennox you were when your brother died?"

I shook my head emphatically. If he only knew . . .

"No, no way. I hope to God I'm miles down the road from *that* me."

"All right, then, it just goes along with what I'm saying. That little-Joe shift checked out a while ago, and now there's a new bunch in you running things."

I looked to see if he was serious. He wasn't smiling, and his hands were unusually still.

The idea intrigued me. If only the Joe-Lennox-who-killed-his-brother crew *had* left. I'd be clean. A whole new me who had had nothing to do with that day . . .

"I'll tell you, all you have to do is look at my wife if you want proof of my theory. She *hates* to think about dying. Christ, she doesn't even like to admit she's sick. But you know what? She loves to read about diseases, especially really rare ones that kill you, like lupus or progeria. And her favorite films in all the world are horror movies. The bloodier the better. Give her a Peter Straub novel and she's in seventh heaven. Now, you cannot tell me the same crew's working inside her. Not unless they're all schizo."

I giggled. "You mean there's different guys in there doing all different things too? Like a football team? You go out for a pass, you block . . ."

"No doubt about it, Joe. Absolutely."

Neither of us said anything for a while, and then I slowly nodded my head. "Maybe you're right. I think my mother was like that."

"What do you mean?"

"She changed all the time. She was a peacock's tail of emotion."

"And you're not like that at all?"

"No, not a tad. I've never been very emotional or flamboyant. Neither has my father."

He winked and smiled devilishly. "You've never done anything out of the ordinary? No disturbing the universe?"

The moment froze like film in a broken projector. It almost started to burn from the middle outward. Paul Tate knew nothing about what had happened with Ross, but suddenly I had the feeling that he did, and it scared me.

"Yes, well sure, sure, I've, uh, I've done some strange things, but—"

"You're beginning to look a wee bit cornered, Joey. It sounds to me as if you've got some dark trunks stored down in your basement." He leered, delighted to know it.

"Uh, Paul, don't get your hopes up too high on that. I ain't no Attila the Hun!"

"That's too bad. Didn't you ever read *Dorian Gray?* Listen to this: 'The only way to get rid of a temptation is to yield to it.' Amen, brother. I bet you Attila the Hun died a happy man."

"Come on, Paul—"

"Don't play footsie, Joe. You know exactly what I mean. There isn't a person on earth who isn't up to their elbows in badness. Why don't you drop the damned façade and admit it?"

"Because I think it's better to move away from it! Get on to other things! And hope we'll be able to do better next time, if we're *given* a next time." I was getting too excited and had to turn my volume down.

"Joe, you are what you've done. You are what you're doing. Okay, we're all trying to do better, but it just isn't that easy, you know. Maybe it'd be better if we just looked what we've done smack in the face and started dealing with it. Maybe instead of always looking forward to tomorrow, trying to ignore what we did yesterday or today, it'd be better if we squared off with our past actions—" He stopped in mid-sentence and looked at me queerly. His face was bloodless, but what really struck me was a kind of terrible stillness in his eyes and on his lips. It was gone in an instant, but it left his face looking drawn and blurred, as if something important had gone out of him, leaving him only half filled.

Ironically, no sooner had I gone to sleep that night than I started dreaming about Ross. As far as I can remember, nothing much happened, yet something scared me awake; it was a long time before I could sleep again. In the dark I looked toward the ceiling and remembered the time he had poured syrup on me. How do you square off with your past actions when you don't know if they were right or wrong?

"Who's that?"

"*Us*, dummy! Can't you tell?"

I sat forward and looked more carefully at the picture on the screen. The people were holding on to the edge of a swimming pool, their hair slicked back and wet from the water. They looked young and exhausted. It really didn't look like either Paul or India. India put the bowl of popcorn on my lap. It was almost empty. We'd been popping and eating it all night.

"Are you bored, Joey? I hate looking at other people's slides. They're about as interesting as looking in someone's mouth."

"No! I love pictures and home movies. It lets you catch up on the part of people's lives you missed."

"Joe Lennox, career diplomat."

Paul pressed the button, and a shot of India came on. It must have been taken shortly after the last one, because she was still in the same swimsuit and her hair was wet-flat on her head. She was smiling to beat the band, and there was no mistaking her loveliness now. She must have been five years younger, but she was the same delightful woman.

"This next one is my father. The only person he ever liked besides my mother was Paul."

"Aw shucks, India."

"Shut up. That's no big compliment. He did *not* like me, his one and only daughter. He thought I was stuck up, which I am, but so what? Next slide, Professor."

"That's when, India? Was I going to Morocco?"

"I don't remember. Great shot though. I forgot all about that picture, Paul. You look good. Very *Foreign Correspondent*-y." She reached back and caressed his knee. I saw him touch her hand in the dark and hold it. How I envied them their love.

The next slide came on, and I blinked in amazement. India and I were standing very close together, her arm through mine, and we were looking intently up at the Ferris wheel at the Prater.

"Me and my spy camera!" Paul reached over and took a handful of popcorn. "I bet neither of you knew I'd taken that one!"

"No, no, you only showed it to me twelve times after you got it back! Next slide."

"Could I have a print of it, Paul?"

"Sure, Joey, no problem."

The painful thought crossed my mind that someday, somewhere far away, the Tates would be showing these same slides to someone else and that someone would ask in an uninterested voice who the guy standing with India was. I know the Buddhists say all transient things suffer, and there were times when that didn't bother me at all. But when it came to Paul and India I wondered, truly, what I would do without them in my life. I knew it would all go on as usual, but I was reminded of people with bad hearts who are told to stop using salt in their diet. Inevitably after a while they come boasting to you that they've given it up completely and don't miss it. So what? Anyone can survive; the purpose of life, however, is not only to survive but to get a little enjoyment out of it while you're at it. I could "live" without salt too, but I wouldn't be happy. Every time I looked at a steak I'd know how much better it would taste if I could only shake a little salt on. The same held with the Tates: life would toodle on okay, but they traveled so easily and joyously through the days, you couldn't help being swept up along with them. It made everything much richer and fuller.

After what had happened in my life, I was torn between being highly suspicious of love and longing for it at the same time. In the short time I had known them, the Tates had unknowingly stormed the walls of my heart and made me run the red flag of love up as high as it would go. When I asked myself if I loved them singly or only as Paul and India/India and Paul, I didn't know. I didn't care, because it wasn't important. I loved them, and that was enough for me.

4

One day out of the blue Paul called and said he was going on a business trip to Hungary and Poland for two weeks. He hated the whole idea but it was necessary, so that was that.

"Joey, the point is that I try to avoid these damned trips because sometimes India gets nervous and down when I'm gone for more than a few days at a shot. You know what I mean? It doesn't always happen, but once in a while she gets, well, skittery . . ." His voice trailed back down into the phone, and there was no sound for several seconds.

"Paul, it's no problem. We'll hang around a lot together. Don't even think about it. What did you think I was going to do, abandon her?"

He sighed, and his voice leaped back up to full strength again—tough and sturdy. "Joey, that's great. You're the kid. I don't even know why I was worried in the first place. I knew you'd take care of her for me."

"Hey, *vuoi un pugno?*"

"What?"

"That's Italian for 'Do you want a punch in the nose?' What kind of friend did you think I was?"

"I know, I know, I'm a dope. But take *really* good care of her, Joey. She's my jewel."

When I hung up, I kept my hand on the back of the receiver. He was off that afternoon, and suddenly I had me a dinner date. I wondered what I should wear. My brand spanking new, hideously expensive Gianni Versace pants. Only the best for India Tate.

The thought crossed my mind while I was dressing that wherever we went for the next two weeks people would think we were a couple. India and Joe. She wore a wedding ring, and if someone saw it they would naturally assume I had given it to her. India and Joseph Lennox. I smiled and looked at myself in the mirror. I began to warble an old James Taylor tune.

India wore cavalry tweed slacks the color of golden fall leaves and a maroon turtleneck sweater. She held my arm wherever we went, and was funny and elegant and better than ever. From the beginning she almost never mentioned Paul, and after a while neither did I.

We ended the first night in a snack bar near Grinzing, where a bunch of punky motorcycle riders kept shooting us murderous looks because we were laughing and having a great time. We made no attempt to conceal our delight. One boy with a shaved head and a dark safety pin through his earlobe looked at me with a thousand pounds of either disgust or envy—I couldn't decipher which. How could anyone as square as me be having so much fun? It was wrong, unfair. After a while the gang strutted out. On the way, the girls all combed their hair and the boys slid gigantic fishtank helmets over their heads with careful, loving slowness.

Later we stood on a street corner across from the café and waited in the fall cold for a tram to take us back downtown. I was freezing in no time at all. Bad circulation. Seeing me shake, India rubbed my arms through my coat. It was a familiar, intimate gesture, and I wondered if she would have done it if Paul had been there. What a ridiculous, small thing to think. It was insulting both to India and to Paul. I was ashamed.

Luckily she started singing, and after a while I got over my guilt and cautiously joined her. We sang "Love Is a Simple Thing" and "Summertime" and "Penny Candy." Feeling pretty sure of myself, I piped up with "Under the Boardwalk," but she said she didn't know that one. Didn't know "Under the Boardwalk"? She looked at me, smiled, and shrugged. I told her it was one of the all-time greats, but she only shrugged again and tried to blow a smoke ring with her warm breath. I told her she had to have it in her repertoire, and that tomorrow night I would cook us dinner and play all my old Drifters records for her. She said that sounded good. In my enthusiasm I didn't realize what I'd done. I had invited her to my apartment alone. Alone. As soon as it hit me, the night suddenly seemed ten degrees colder. When she looked down the track for the tram, I let my teeth chatter. *Alone.* I stuck my hands deep into my pockets and felt as stretched as a rubber band wrapped around a thousand fat playing cards.

Why was I so scared to have her over alone? Nothing happened the next night. We ate spaghetti carbonara and

drank Chianti and listened to the Joseph Lennox Golden
Oldies Hit Parade of records. Everything was very honorable
and aboveboard, and I ended up feeling a bit blue afterward.
Since my relationship with the two of them had deepened,
my initial desire for India had dwindled, but after she left
my apartment that night, I looked at my hands and knew
that I would have made love to her in a second if the right
situation had come up. I felt like a shit and an A-prime be-
trayer for thinking that, but, Christ, who says no to an India
Tate? Eunuchs, madmen, or saints. None of the above
being me.

I didn't see her the next day, although we talked for a
long time over the phone. She was going to the opera with
some friends and kept telling me how much she liked
Mahler's *The Three Pintos*. I wanted to tell her before we
hung up how disappointed I was that I wouldn't be seeing
her that day, but I didn't.

Something very strange and almost more intimate than
sex happened the next day. *How* it happened is so utterly
ludicrous I'm embarrassed to explain. India later said it was
a great scene out of a bad movie, but I still felt it was the
worst kind of corn.

It was Saturday night; she was cooking dinner for us at
their apartment. While she moved around her kitchen cutting and chopping and stirring, I started singing. She joined
in, and we went through "Camelot," "Yesterday," and
"Guess Who I Saw Today, My Dear?" So far, so good. She
was still cutting and chopping; I had my arms behind my
head, looking at the ceiling and feeling warm and content.
When we finished "He Loves and She Loves," I waited a
few seconds to see if she was going to volunteer one. When
she didn't, I sang the first few bars of "Once Upon a Time."
Why that song I still don't know, because it usually surfaces
only when I'm depressed or sad. She had a nice high voice
that reminded me of light blue. She could also move it
around mine and do some lovely harmonizing. It made me

feel about a hundred times more musical than I was, so long as I stayed on my notes.

We got three quarters of the way through the song, but then the end loomed up. If you don't know the tune, I should tell you that the end is very sad; I always stop singing before I get there. This time I'd arrived, but because she was there with me, I decided to mumble my way through to the finish. It did no good, because she dropped off too, and we were stuck out there in space with nowhere to go. All of a sudden I felt sad and full of tired echoes, and my eyes filled with tears. I knew I would start crying if I didn't think of something fast. Here I was in my friends' warm kitchen, the man of her house for a few hours. Something I had wanted for years but had never been able to find. There had been women before—deer and mice and lions. There had been moments when I was sure—but they weren't. Or they'd been convinced, but I wasn't . . . and it was never simple or good. What it boiled down to was being alone—particularly alone—in Vienna in the middle of my twenties and, worst of all, growing used to it.

My eyes were stuck on the ceiling while the black silence honked its horn, but I knew I would have to look at her soon. Steeling myself, I blinked three or four times against the tears and slowly brought my scared eyes down. She was leaning against a counter and had both hands in her pants pockets. She'd held nothing back, and although she was crying, she looked at me with a grave, loving stare.

She walked over and sat down on my knee. Putting her long arms around my neck, she hugged me tightly. When I returned the embrace—tentatively and light with fear—she spoke into my neck.

"Sometimes in the middle of everything I get so *sad.*"

I nodded and began rocking us back and forth in the chair. A father and his scared child.

"Oh, Joe, I just get so spooked."

"Of what? You want to talk?"

"Of nothing. Everything. Getting old, knowing nothing. Never being on the cover of *Time* magazine."

I laughed and squeezed her harder. I knew exactly what she meant.

"The beans are burning."

"I know. I don't care. Keep hugging me. It's better than beans."

"You wanna go out for hamburgers?"

She pulled back and smiled at me. Her face was all tears. She sniffled and rubbed her nose. "Can we?"

"Yes, honey, and you can have a milkshake too, if you want."

"Joey, you're breaking my heart. You're a good fellow."

"You did that to me once, so we're even now."

"Did what?" She let go and started to get up.

"Broke my heart." I kissed her on the top of the head and smelled that fine clean India smell again.

The next morning we had breakfast at a brass and marble *Konditorei* on Porzellangasse, near their apartment. Then, because the day was bright and clear, we decided to drive up along the Danube and stop when we saw a nice place. Both of us felt full of life and were definitely in the mood for a long walk. We found a spot near Tulln, a dirt path that ran parallel to the river and wound in and out of the forest. She held my hand the whole way, and we walked and ran and waved at the crew of a Rumanian barge that was slowly working its way upstream. When someone on board saw us and tooted the horn, we looked at each other wonderingly, as if we had accomplished something magical. It was the kind of day that, in retrospect, is almost cheapened by its clichés, but that, when you're experiencing it, has an innocence and clarity that can't ever be matched in your more rational times.

We drove back to town under a plum and orange sunset

and had an early dinner at a Greek restaurant near the university. The food was terrible, but the company was something special.

The two weeks Paul was gone went by like that. I didn't do a lick of work because we were constantly together. We cooked, went for walks in remote districts of town where no one ever went, much less sightseers. The fact that we were probably the only people who had ever gone there *to* sightsee pleased us no end. We went to a couple of movies in German, and on the spur of the moment to hear Alfred Brendel playing Brahms at the Konzerthaus.

One night we decided to see what Vienna offered in the way of night life. We must have gone to twenty places and had thirty cups of coffee, ten glasses of wine, and a Coke here and there. At two in the morning we were in the Café Hawelka looking at all the phonies when India turned to me and said, "Joey, you're the most fun man I've been with since Paul. Why can't I marry both of you?"

Paul was due in on Saturday night; the two of us planned to go down to the train station to meet him. I didn't want to tell her, but for the first time since I had known him, I wasn't looking forward to seeing Paul all that much. Call it greed or possessiveness or whatever, I had grown used to squiring India around town on my arm, and it was going to be damned hard and sad to have to give it up.

"Hi ya, kids!"

We watched him zoom down the platform toward us, arms full of bags and packages, a great beaming smile on his face. He hugged India and then me. He had a thousand stories to tell about "the Commies" and insisted we go to a café so he could have a real cup of coffee for the first time in two weeks. He let me carry one of his suitcases, which seemed to be light as air. I didn't know if it was empty or because adrenaline was pumping through my body a mile a minute. I didn't know how I felt anymore. India walked between us, holding us each by the arm. She looked completely happy.

"That crumb."

"India, take it easy."

"No! That dirty crumb. How do you like that? He actually asked."

"What exactly did he say?"

"He *asked* me if we'd slept together."

Big Ben tolled in the middle of my stomach. Half because of indignation, half because with one question Paul had put his finger right on the button. Had I wanted to sleep with India? Yes. Did I still want to sleep with India, my one best friend who was married to my other best friend? Yes.

"And you said?"

"What do you *think* I said? No! He's never done that before." She was fuming. A few more degrees and smoke would have come out of her ears.

"India?"

"What?"

"Never mind."

"*What?* Say it. I hate that. Tell me now."

"It's nothing."

"Joe, if you don't tell me, I'll kill you!"

"I wanted to."

"Wanted to what?"

"Go to bed with you."

"Uh oh."

"I told you, you should forget it."

"I'm not uh-ohing because of that." She clapped her hands together and held them tight against her stomach. "The night we went to the cafés together I wanted you so much I thought I was going to die."

"Uh oh."
"You said it, brother. Now what?"

We talked and talked and talked and talked, until we were exhausted. She suggested we go out and do some shopping. I followed her around the market, my knees shaking the whole time. Once in a while, weighing a grapefruit or choosing eggs, she threw me a look that sent me reeling. This was bad. The whole thing was bad. Black. Wrong. What could you do?

She picked up a triangle of Brie cheese. "Are you think-ing?"

"Too much. My head's going to blow a fuse."

"Mine too. You like Brie?"

"Huh?"

Paul called that night around seven and asked if I wanted to go to a horror film with them. It was exactly what I didn't want to do, and I begged off. When I hung up, I wondered if my refusal would make him suspicious. He knew India and I got together once in a while during the day. We would rendezvous when she was through painting or after one of her German classes at the university. What would happen now? He was so kind and generous; I'd never thought of Paul as a jealous or suspicious man. Was this a glimpse of that side of him?

"Joe?"

"India? What time is it, for Christ's sake?" I tried to make out the numbers on the clock next to the bed, but my eyes were too fogged over from sleep.

"It's after three. Were you asleep?"

"Uh, yes. Where are you?"

"Out walking around. Paul and I had a fight."

"Uh oh. Why are you walking around?" I sat up in bed. The blanket slipped down my chest, and I felt the cold of the room.

"Because I don't want to be home. You wanna have a cup of coffee or something?"

"Well ... uh ... okay. Um, or would you like to come over here? Is that okay?"

"Sure. I'm right at the corner of your street. You know that phone booth?"

I smiled and shook my head. "Should I turn the light on and off three times to signal when the coast is clear?"

I heard the zazzy sound of a Brooklyn raspberry come through the phone before she hung up on me.

"Where'd you get that robe? You look like Margaret Rutherford."

"India, it's three o'clock in the morning. Shouldn't you call Paul?"

"Why? He's not around. He took off."

I was heading toward the kitchen, but that stopped me fast enough. "Took off where?"

"How should I know? He went one way, and I went the other."

"You mean he hasn't actually *gone* anywhere—"

"Joe, shut up. What are we going to do?"

"About this? About you and me? I don't know."

"You really want to go to bed with me?"

"Yes."

She sighed loudly and dramatically. I wanted to look at her, but I couldn't. All my courage had fled with her question.

"Well, Joey, me too, so I guess we got big problems, huh?"

"I guess."

The phone rang. I looked at her and pointed to it. She shook her head. "I ain't answering that, the creep. If it's him, tell him I'm not here. No, no! Tell him I'm in bed with you and can't be disturbed. Ha! That's it! Give it to him!"

"Hello?"

"Joe? Is India there?" His voice said he knew she was but was asking just to be polite.

I wasn't taking any chances with my answer. "Yes, Paul. She *just* got here. One second."

This time I held the receiver out to her, and after a dirty look, she snatched it out of my hand. "*What,* stinko? Huh? Yes, you're damned right! What? Yes. All right . . . What? . . . I said all right, Paul. Okay." She hung up. "Ratface."

"Well?"

"Well, he said he was sorry and wants to apologize. I don't know if I should let him." She said it while she buttoned up her coat. She stopped when her hands got to the last one, and then she looked me long and hard in the eyes. "Joe, I'm going home and listen to my husband apologize. He said he even wants to apologize to you. Christ! This thing's going to happen and we both know it and I'm going home to listen to him apologize to *me* for being suspicious. Is it bad, Joe? Are we really this bad?"

We looked at each other, and it was a long time before I realized my teeth were actually chattering.

"You're scared, huh, Joe?"

"Yes."

"Me too. Me too. Good night."

Two weeks later I turned her wet face to me and kissed her. It was exactly, *exactly* the way I'd envisioned India Tate kissing: gently, simply, but with a delicious intensity.

She took my hand and led me into the bedroom. The big

goose-down comforter was folded neatly across the foot of my double bed. It was coral pink; the bottom sheet was white and without wrinkles. The glass lamps on the side tables gave off a muted, intimate glow. She walked to the other side of the bed and began unbuttoning her shirt. In a minute I saw she was wearing no bra, which must have embarrassed her, because she turned away and finished with her back to me.

"Joe, can I turn out the light?"

In bed I discovered that her breasts were larger than I'd thought; her skin was tight and firm everywhere. In the dark it was a dancer's body, very warm against the fresh, icy sheets.

I don't know if sex is a reflection of a person's true spirit or personality, although I've heard it said often enough. India was very good—very fluid and active. She knew how to prolong both of our orgasms without making it feel as if she was manipulating or trying to remember some page out of *The Joy of Sex.* She said she wanted to feel me as deep inside her as possible, and when I was there, she rewarded me with words and shivers that made me want to plunge even deeper and rattle every object on her shelves.

We moved quickly through the first and then the less shrill, less desperate second. That, however, was nothing new: for me the first time with any woman has inevitably been more to prove it's actually happening than to enjoy. Once you've passed that barrier, you become human and fallible and tender again.

A street lamp threw its harsh, cheap light across the bed. India came back into the room holding two small glasses of the wine I had bought that afternoon. She was still naked, and when she sat down next to me on the edge of the bed, the light moved up her side and stopped just below her breasts.

"It's very cold. I took a big sip in the kitchen and it gave me one of those ice-cream headaches." She handed me one, and after I sat up, we touched glasses in a quiet, unspoken toast.

"Aren't you cold?"

"No, I'm fine."

"That's right—neither of you—oops." I was so embarrassed I closed my eyes. The last thing I wanted was to bring Paul into the room.

"Joey, it's okay. He's not here." She drank her wine and looked out the window. "I'm still glad we did it, and that's supposed to be the big test, isn't it? I mean, after you've zipped through the passion and are back where you started? I wanted you, it happened, and now we're here and still happy, right? I don't want to think about anything else. I have to tell you something even though it doesn't mean a thing. I've never done this with anyone since Paul, okay? It doesn't matter, but I wanted you to know."

She reached out and ran her still-warm palm down my chest. She caught the top of the blanket with her fingers and pulled it down: past my stomach, past my penis, which was blooming again like an African violet. She straddled me and, licking her fingertips, reached down and spread the wetness over the head. Then she took hold of it, strongly— like a gun—and slid it into her. Halfway there she stopped, and I was afraid it had hurt her, but I saw she was only trying to hold the moment until she was ready to own it again.

One day in bed we had a conversation about my "type" of woman.

"I bet you I'm not your kind, am I?"

"What do you mean?" I pulled the pillow under my head.

"I mean, I'm not your type of girl. Woman."

"India, you must be or else we wouldn't be here, would we?" I patted the bed between us.

"Oh, yeah, sure, I'm good-looking and all, but I'm not your kind of girl. No, no, you don't have to say anything. Sssh, wait a minute—let me try and guess."

"India—"

"No, shut up. I want to try this. Knowing you ... you probably like big blondes or redheads with tiny fannies and big boobs."

"Wrong! Don't be so smirky, smart aleck. I do like blondes, but I've never been a big-breast man. If you really want to know the truth, I like beautiful legs. You have beautiful legs, you know."

"Yeah, they're okay. Are you sure about that breast thing? I would've sworn you were a tight-sweater lad."

"Nope, I like long sleek legs. Most of all, I'm crazy for a woman who's at ease with her looks, if you know what I mean. She doesn't wear much makeup because it doesn't mean anything to her. If she's attractive she knows it, and that's enough. She doesn't feel the need to show off what she's got."

"And she bakes her own bread, believes in natural childbirth, and eats three bowls of granola a day."

"India, you asked. You're making me sound stupid."

"Sorry." She slid over in bed and put one of those long legs over mine. "Besides looks, what else do you like about me?"

She was serious, so I answered seriously. "You're unpredictable. You're good-looking too, but behind those looks are all these different women, and I like that very much. Everyone has different qualities if they're at all interesting, but in your case it's as if there's no one India Tate. I think it's amazing. When I'm with you, I feel as if I'm with ten women."

She tickled me. "Sometimes you get so serious, Joey. You look as if I just asked you a question in biochemistry. Come over here and give me a big smooch."

I did, and we lay quietly in each other's arms.

"Can I tell you something crazy, India? Part of me always looks forward to seeing Paul. Is that nuts?"

She kissed my forehead. "Not at all. He's your friend. Why shouldn't you like seeing him? I think it's nice."

"Yes, but it's like that old story about why murderers put out their victims' eyes after they've killed them."

She pushed me away, and her voice was testy. "What are you *talking* about?"

"You see, there's this old superstition that the last thing a dead person sees is the guy who's done him in, if he was killed from in front, see? So some people used to think that since that was so, the image would register on the dead man's eyeballs like a photograph. Look at the guy's eyes and you'll see who did it." I stopped and tried to smile at her; only it turned out to be a forlorn, useless smile. "I keep thinking that one day Paul is going to look in my eyes and see you there."

"You're saying I murdered you?" Her face showed nothing: it was only pale and delicate. Her voice was as distant as the moon. I wanted to touch her, but I didn't.

"No, India, that's not what I'm saying at all."

In those first days of our affair, I kept watching her as intently when we made love as a prospector looking at a geiger counter, but there was nothing in her expression I hadn't already seen. I think I was hoping that, in the midst of that full but simple passion that took place every time we pulled down the sheets, there would be a hint or a clue as to what was happening between her and Paul. And I didn't even know what I was hoping for. Did I want everything to be the way it had always been? Or did I secretly, selfishly, wish she was disenchanted with her husband and would end up wanting me?

How long would it be before he found out? When it came to trysts, rendezvous, and love messages written in invisible ink, I wasn't very subtle or capable. It had happened once or twice in the past. My way of dealing with it then had been to let the woman decide when and where and how; I would go along with it no matter how urgently I felt I needed to be with her. As far as that was concerned, I knew my limits and knew if I ever tried to run the affair I'd botch everything in two seconds flat.

Paul was good old Paul and treated me no differently. India was the same too; only once in a while she would wink or give my foot a tiny tap under the table. I was the only one who was different; I was "on" every time we were together. But they both affected not to notice.

In the meantime, India continued to come over, and we had our slivers of time when the world was only as big as my bed. When she was there I tried to put everything out of my mind and seize the part of the day she could give me. It was not a difficult time either, but I was often surprised by how exhausted I was at night. I would often fall into bed with a hunger for sleep I'd never known before. One day, when I asked India if the same thing had been happening to her, she was already asleep on my arm; it was only ten o'clock in the morning.

Around the beginning of November, guilt began to whistle a familiar tune. Hard as I tried, I couldn't stop it. I knew a great part stemmed from my ambivalent feelings toward India. Did I love her? No, I didn't. When we made love she often said things like "Love-yes! Love-oh!" and even then I felt uncomfortable, because I knew I didn't love her. As far as I was concerned that was all right, because I cared for her, wanted her, and needed her in many different, ever-increasing ways. I had long ago given up on the possibility of finding someone I could love totally and endlessly. Sometimes I tried to convince myself that what I felt for India was the *only* kind of love Joseph Lennox could ever feel, but I knew I was lying. But what more did I want? What ingredient was missing? I had no idea, except that where there should have been magic and blue sparks, there was "only" great sleight-of-hand or a brilliant trick I loved but knew was done with little hidden mirrors.

5

Holding a bouquet of flowers in front of me like a delicate shield, I waited for someone to open the door.

India appeared and smiled at the cluster of red and pink roses. "Well, Joey, that's mighty neighborly of you." She took them and gave me a buss on the cheek. I started through the door and suddenly felt a bitter little pinch in the middle of my back. India loved to pinch. "You look great tonight, sporty. If Paul wasn't here, I'd throw you down on the floor and ravish you."

That was enough to shoot me forward into their living room. I wasn't in the mood to live dangerously. Paul was nowhere to be seen, so I assumed he was in the kitchen preparing his part of the dinner. They liked to do it that way— Paul was soup and salad chef, India main course and dessert. The room was warm and hummed with an apricot light. I sat on the couch and put my nervous hands on my nervous knees.

"What are you drinking, Joey?" Paul came out of the kitchen with a bottle of vinegar in one hand and a beer in the other.

"That beer looks good."

"Beer? You don't drink beer."

"No, well, once in a while." I laughed and tried to sound like a debonair character out of a 1930s movie. Herbert Marshall. Ha ha—very suave.

"Okay, beer it is. I also want you to know, bub, that this meal tonight is going to outdo Paul Bocuse. Beginning with salad niçoise, no less. Fresh anchovies too; none of them little tinned babies!" He went back to the kitchen and left me to ponder slim gray anchovies. Ross had once made me eat two big tins of them, which didn't increase my appreciation any. It was either that or he'd tell Bobby Hanley about my misuse of his sister. Now my hands wilted on my knees as I wondered what I could do to keep the damned things in my stomach once they'd arrived.

"I'll eat lots of bread."

"Huh?" India came into the room with the flowers in a yellow vase full of water. She placed it in the middle of the table and stood back to admire them. "Where did you get roses at this time of the year? They must have cost you a fortune!"

I was still working on anchovy digestion and didn't answer.

"Paul is really putting on the dog for you tonight, Joe."

He stuck his head out of the kitchen. "You're damned right. We owe him for about nine meals. Christ, he had to take care of you for two weeks! That'd be enough to drive Sister Teresa around the bend. *India* wanted to have fried chicken and mashed potatoes."

"Shut up, Paul. Joe likes fried chicken."

"Low level, India, very low level. Wait till he sees what I've got for him." He started counting off on his fingers. "Salad niçoise. *Coq au vin.* Pineapple upside-down cake."

I had to stop myself from physically recoiling into the couch. I detested every one of those things. I hadn't eaten any of them, thank God, since my mother had gone away so many years before. In fact, Ross and I had once made lists of our most unfavorite of her dishes, and Paul's menu for tonight had about half of mine. I managed—just—to put an idiotic lip-smackin' smile on my face that pleased him.

India and I made small talk while he banged away in the other room. She looked so different. She wore her hair up, accentuating the high patrician lines of her face. She moved gracefully around the room, sure and at ease in her surroundings. I felt like Jekyll and Hyde here. On this couch I'd had long talks with Paul. Over by the window I had once slipped my hands into the back pockets of India's blue jeans and pulled her close to me. At the dining table, now set with pinks and tropical green, we'd sat and had coffee in the middle of an afternoon and talked. The window, the table—the room was full of ghosts so recent I could almost reach out and touch them. Yet in a part of my heart I felt smug and content because they were half mine.

"Soup's on!" Paul staggered playfully out of the kitchen with a big wooden salad bowl. Two wooden forks stuck up from either side like brown rabbit ears.

I tried to talk straight through each course. I avoided looking down at my plate as much as possible. It reminded me of a time I had climbed a small mountain and discovered halfway up that I was petrified of heights. A friend who had come along told me everything would be all right so long as I didn't look down. That advice had gotten me through more than one scrape in my life, not all of them associated with mountains.

Miraculously, there were only a few suspicious smudges of pineapple on my plate when I finally peeked; the worst was over, and I could put my tired fork down with a clear conscience.

Paul asked who was for coffee and disappeared again into the kitchen. India was sitting on my right; she gave me a little jab in the hand with her dessert fork.

"You look as if you just ate a tire."

"Sssh! I hate anchovies."

"Why didn't you say so?"

"Sssh, India!"

She shook her head. "You're such a dope."

"India, stop! I'm not a dope. If he'd gone to all that trouble to cook—"

The lights went out, and a table with candles on each of the four corners came gliding in from the kitchen. They illuminated Paul's face; I saw he was wearing his Little Boy top hat.

A trumpet fanfare and a blasting drum roll followed.

"Ladies and gentlemen, for your after-dinner enjoyment, the Hapsburg Room would like to present the Amazing Little Boy and his bag, or should I say *hat*, full of tricks!"

Paul remained deadpan throughout the introduction. When it was over (I assumed it came from a tape recorder in the other room), he bowed deeply and reached behind him. The lights in the room came on again, and at the same instant the candles went out. Poof! Just like that.

"Hey, Paul, that's a great trick!"

He nodded, but put a finger to his lips for silence. He had on the familiar white gloves from India's *Little Boy* painting and a cutaway jacket over a white T-shirt. Taking off the hat, he placed it rim up on the table directly in front of him. I looked at India, but she was watching the performance.

From inside his jacket he took out a large silver key. He held it up for us to see and then dropped it into the silk hat. A burst of flame shot upward, and I jumped in my seat. He smiled and, picking up the hat, turned it so we could see down into it. A small black bird swooped out and winged over to our table. It landed on India's dessert plate and pecked at a piece of cake. Paul tapped the table twice; the bird flew obediently back to him. Placing the hat over it, Paul made a loud kissing noise and pulled the hat up again. Twenty or thirty silver keys fell out of it with a metallic clatter.

India began clapping furiously. I joined right in.

"Bravo, Boy!"

"Paul, my God, that's fantastic!" I'd had no idea he was so talented. "But where's the bird?"

He slowly shook his head and put his finger again to his lips. I felt like the bad seven-year-old at the second-grade puppet show.

"Do your mind reading, Boy!"

Although I didn't believe in it, just the idea of Paul reading my mind at that point made me uncomfortable. I wanted to give India a belt in the mouth to keep her quiet.

"Little Boy is not reading minds tonight. Return another time and he will tell all, including Joseph Lennox's vast unhappiness with tonight's dinner!"

"No, come on, Paul—"

"Another time!" He moved his arm through the air as if he were pushing a curtain across an invisible window.

One white hand stopped above the rim of the silk hat. Paul made the kissing sound again, and the blade of orange flame burst up for the second time that night. It disappeared in an instant, and the hat toppled over on its side. There was a tinny, *clinkety-clink* sound, and out hopped a large toy tin bird. It was black, with a yellow beak and black wings, and a big red key in its back. It slowly goose-stepped to the edge of the table and stopped. Paul snapped his fingers, but nothing happened. He snapped them again. The toy rose off the table and began to fly. It flapped its wings too slowly and cautiously: an old man getting into a cold swimming pool. That didn't matter, because slow or not, it glided up and off the table and flew in a loud putter around the room.

"Jesus Christ! Amazing!"

"Yay, Little Boy!"

The bird was at the window, hovering at the venetian blinds in a way that made it look as if it was having a look outside. Paul tapped the table. The bird turned reluctantly and flew back to him. When it landed, Paul once again covered it with the hat. I started to clap, but India touched my arm and shook her head—there was more, the trick wasn't

over. Paul smiled and turned the hat rim up again. He gave
it the familiar two taps; the flame shot up for the third time.
This time it didn't stop. Instead, Paul turned the hat over,
and out tumbled a screeching, burning, live bird—a small
package of fire that kept trying to stand up or fly . . . I was so
aghast I didn't know what to do.

"Paul, stop!"

"My name is Little Boy!"

"Paul, for godsake!"

India grabbed my arm so hard it hurt. "Boy! Call him
Little Boy or he'll never stop!"

"Little Boy! Little Boy! Stop it! What the hell are you
trying to do?"

The bird continued to screech. I gaped at Paul, he smiled
back. He casually picked up the hat and placed it over the
staggering flame. He tapped the top and pulled the whole
thing up and away. Nothing. No bird, no smoke, smell,
ashes . . . Nothing.

I realized after some seconds that India was clapping.

"Bra-vo, Boy! Won-derful!"

I looked at her. She was having the time of her life.

Little Boy reappeared on Thanksgiving Day. I hadn't had
turkey or cranberry sauce in years, so when India discovered
that the Vienna Hilton served a special Thanksgiving dinner
in one of its innumerable restaurants, we all agreed to go.

Paul had the day off and wanted to take full advantage of
it. I would write until noon; then we would meet for coffee
at the Hotel Europa.

After that we'd ramble around the First District and look
at the fancy store windows. Then slowly we'd make our way
over to the Hilton for a drink at the Klimt bar, and on to the
big meal.

I got there a little late; they were standing in front of the hotel. They both had on light spring jackets that looked ridiculous in the midst of other people's fur coats, gloves, and an insistent winter wind. Both were dressed casually, except that Paul was holding the big leather briefcase he took to work. I assumed he'd been to his office for something that morning.

The Graben and Kärntner strasse were alive with well-dressed, well-to-do people promenading from store to store. Everything in that part of town costs more than it should, but the Viennese love prestige and you often see the most surprising people wearing Missoni clothes or carrying Louis Vuitton handbags.

"There he is, Shoeless Joe from Hannibal, Mo."

"Hi! Have you been waiting long?"

Paul shook his head no, India nodded yes. They looked at each other and smiled.

"I'm sorry, but I got all caught up with work."

"Yeah? Well, let's get caught up on some coffee. My stomach's beginning to hiss." India marched off, leaving the two of us in the dust. She did that sometimes. I once saw them from afar walking "together." It was ludicrous; she was at least three feet ahead of him, striding and looking straight ahead like a serious military cadet. Paul stayed within a few feet of her wake, but he swiveled his head from side to side, taking in everything and in no hurry whatsoever. I followed them for a few blocks, feeling wonderfully voyeuristic, anxious to see when India would turn around and give him a blast to get going. She never did. She marched, he dawdled.

Our coffee went well. Paul had been to the airport the day before and described the passengers disembarking from a charter flight from New York. He said he could immediately tell who was who because all the Austrian women were dressed to the nines in chic new designer clothes, while their men favored tight new jeans and cowboy boots that ranged in color from sand to plum with black fleur-de-lis designs. All of them came down the ramp fast and assured, smiling because they knew the territory.

In contrast, the Americans on the flight were dressed in drably practical shoes with thick crepe bottoms and drip-dry clothes so stiff and unyielding that they made the people look as if they were all walking between sandwich-board advertisements. They came into the airport slowly, with dismayed or angry looks. Suspicious eighty-year-olds who had just landed on the moon.

Some stores on the Graben had already begun their Christmas push and I wondered when the men would come in from the country farms with Christmas trees for sale. The Austrian tradition is not to decorate your tree until Christmas Eve, but they are for sale weeks before.

"What do you do at Christmas, Joey?"

"It depends. I've stayed around here. Once I went over to Salzburg to see how they'd done it up. It's something you two should see if you haven't already— That town at Christmastime is something."

They glanced at each other, and India shrugged indifferently. I wondered if she was mad at me for some reason. After coffee, we walked toward St. Stephen's Cathedral; I put my gloves on. I was sure it was getting colder, but neither of them showed any sign of it. They were dressed for a day in late spring.

The restaurant was surprisingly full. Paul nodded to people at several tables while the hostess led us to ours. It was close to a large picture window that gave a full view of the Stadtpark and the purple puff clouds that hung, unmoving, over it.

"The reason why I asked before about what you're doing over the holidays, Joey, is because we're going to Italy for five days and wanted to know if you'd like to come with us?"

I zapped a look at India, but her face said nothing. Where had this come from? Whose idea was it? I didn't know what the hell I was supposed to say. I opened my mouth twice like a hungry fish, but nothing came out.

"Is that supposed to mean yes?"

"Yes, I guess . . . Sure, yes!" I fiddled with my napkin. It fell on the floor. When I bent down to get it, I pulled a muscle in my back. It hurt. I tried to get my mind to race into every corner at once to find out what was going on here. India sure wasn't helping much.

"That's great. Well, now that we've got that settled, you kids'll have to excuse me for a minute. I'll be back in two shakes." Paul got up, briefcase in hand, and headed out of the room.

I watched until I heard the crunch of celery in my ear. I turned to see India pointing a long green stalk at me.

"Don't you *dare* ask me how it happened, Joe. The whole thing was his idea. He woke up this morning in a big lather and wanted to know what I thought of it. What could I say? No? Maybe he thinks he's doing penance or something for being suspicious of you before."

"I don't know. It gives me the willies."

"You and me both, Joe. But I don't want to talk about it today. It's far away, and a lot can happen. Let's eat lots of turkey now and be happy."

"That might be a little difficult." I nervously wiped my mouth with my napkin.

"Quiet! I want you to tell me what the Lennox family used to do for Thanksgiving. Did you guys eat turkey?"

"No, as a matter of fact. My brother, Ross, didn't like it, so we had goose instead."

"Goose? Whoever heard of eating goose on Thanksgiving? That Ross sounds like a real weirdo, Joe."

"Weirdo? It's not the right word for him. He . . . Do you know you ask about him a lot, India?"

"Yep. Does it bother you? You want to know why? Because he sounds like an interesting demon." She smiled and plucked an olive off my plate.

"Do you like demons?"

"Only if they're interesting." She took another olive off my plate. "Do you know that line from Isak Dinesen: 'It is a moving thing to work together with a demon'?"

The waiter brought the salad, which cut off the rest of whatever else she was going to say. We ate for a while, and then she put down her fork and continued.

"Paul was a little demon when we first met. It's amazing, huh? It's true though. He had hundreds of unpaid traffic tickets, and he used to shoplift with the coolest expression on his face you ever saw."

"Paul? Steal?"

"That's right."

"I can't believe it. My brother used to shoplift too. He once stole all our presents for Christmas."

"Really? How marvelous! See, he was interesting! I'll tell you something else too—you describe him with the most mixed emotions I've ever heard. One day he sounds like your hero, and the next you make him out to be Jack the Ripper."

We talked about it. The main course came, and the waiter asked if he should serve Paul's too or wait until he returned. I looked at my watch and with a jolt realized how long he had been gone. I looked at India to see if she was worried. She pushed the turkey around her plate for a few seconds, then looked at me.

"Joe, it's silly, but would you go to the bathroom and take a look? Everything is okay, I'm sure, but do it for me, would you?"

I put my napkin down and hastily brushed some crumbs off the front of my pants. "Sure! Don't, uh, don't let the waiter eat my turkey, okay?" I said it lightly, hoping she'd smile. But the look on her face was a kind of limbo between concern and exaggerated ease.

I was up, but I didn't want to go. I didn't want to move from the spot. I would have stood there happily in the middle of the restaurant, in front of all those people, for the rest of the day. Dread has no dignity.

Admittedly, since my brother's death terror was as much a part of me as anything else. I was forever quick to jump to conclusions, and often imagined the most awful thing that could occur in any given situation. That was because if I was wrong and it turned out to be nothing, then I would be delighted. If I was right (which was rarely), then the horror could no longer strike me with as much force as it had when Ross died.

I tried not to walk too quickly, both for India's peace of mind (if she happened to be watching) and so as not to draw the eyes of anyone around us. I stared straight ahead, but saw nothing. The thousand clanks of forks on plates and knives on spoons was louder and more alarming than I had ever realized. It drowned out the slip of my feet crossing the carpet and all the noises I make and am so aware of when I'm frightened and am moving toward whatever it is that's frightening me.

At the last minute I stumbled on a bumpy part of the carpet and only just regained my balance. The men's room was directly across from the restaurant in a darkened alcove lit only by a green HERREN sign above the door. I touched the cold metal knob and closed my eyes. I took a gigantic breath and pushed it open. I looked down the line of glistening white urinals. Paul wasn't there. I let out the breath. The room was unnaturally bright and smelled strongly of pine disinfectant. Three gray toilet stalls faced a line of white sinks on the far side of the urinals.

I called his name while I walked toward them. There was no answer. A dismal fear began to take hold of me again, although rationally I knew he could be in any of a hundred different places: making a long telephone call, browsing by the magazine rack . . .

"Paul?"

I saw something move beneath the door of the middle

stall and, without thinking, fell to my knees to see what it was.

For a moment I was sure I recognized his beat-up black loafers, but then the legs rose slowly up and out of view—as if whoever was in there had pulled them to his chest for some bizarre reason. The thought rushed in and out of my mind that I should slide closer to the stall so I could see, but a remnant of the saner me prevailed and wailed that I should get the hell out of there and stop looking under toilet doors.

"Everybody out there has to sit down!"

"Paul?"

"No Paul! Little Boy is here! If you want to stay for the show, you have to play with Little Boy!"

I didn't know what to do. I was down on my knees looking up at the toilet door. A black top hat rose from behind it. Then Paul's face, framed by his two open hands (palms facing outward, thumbs under his chin). He was wearing his Little Boy gloves.

"We have called you all here today to find the answer to the Big Question: Why is Joseph Lennox fucking India Tate?" He looked down at me sweetly. I closed my eyes and saw the blood beating fast behind the lids.

"No one wants to answer? Aw, come on, gang. Boy puts on a whole magic show for you, and you won't answer his one little teeny question?"

I mustered the courage to look at him again. His eyes were closed, but his mouth still moved, talking silently.

Then, "Ha! If no one's going to volunteer, I'll just have to call on you, that's all. Joseph Lennox in the third row! Will you tell us why Joseph Lennox is fucking Paul Tate's wife?"

"Paul—"

"*Not* Paul! Little Boy! Paul isn't with us tonight. He's out somewhere going crazy."

The outside door whooshed open; a man in a gray suit came in. Paul ducked down into the stall, and I stupidly pretended to be tying my shoe. The man ignored me after a fast glance. He tucked in his shirt, straightened his tie, and went out. I watched him leave. When I turned back, Paul was there again, smiling down at me. This time he was resting his elbows on top of the metal door, his chin propped on his crossed white hands. In any other situation he would have looked cute. His head began to move from side to side, slowly and exactly, like a metronome pendulum to the beat.

> "In-dia and Joe, sittin' in a tree
> K-I-S-S-I-N-G!"

He said it two or three times. I didn't know what to do, where to go. What was I supposed to do? The smile fell away, and he pursed his lips. "Joey, I'd never have done it to you." His voice was soft as a prayer in church. *"Never!* Goddamn you! Get out! Get out of my fucking life! Bastard. You'd have gone with us to Italy! You'd've fucked her there, too! Get out!"

I think he was crying. I couldn't look. I ran.

6

Two miserable days later I was still trying to figure out what to do when the telephone rang. I looked at it for three full rings before I picked it up.

"Joe?" It was India. Her voice was scared, haunted.

"India? Hi."

"Joe, Paul's dead."

"*Dead?* What? What are you talking about?"

"He's *dead,* goddamn it! What do you think I mean? The

ambulance men just came and took him away. He's gone. He's dead!" She started crying. Big, startling sobs, broken only by gasps for breath.

"Oh, my God! *How?* What happened?"

"His heart. He had a heart attack. He was doing his exercises and he just fell on the floor. I thought he was kidding. But he's dead, Joe. Oh, my God, what am I going to do? Joe, you're the only person I could call. What am I going to do?"

"I'll be there in half an hour. Less. India, don't do anything until I get there."

No one ever gets used to death. Soldiers, doctors, morticians see it continually and grow accustomed to a part or a facet of it, but not the whole thing. I don't think anyone could. To me, being told of the death of someone I knew well is like walking down a familiar staircase in the dark. You know from a million times on it just how many steps there are to the bottom, but then your foot moves to touch the next one ... and it's not there. Stumbling, you can't believe it. And you will often stumble there from now on because, as with all things you know by habit, you've used that lost step so many times the two of you are inseparable.

Rushing down the staircase of my building, I kept testing (or was it tasting?) the words, like an actor trying to get his new lines straight. "Paul's *dead?*" "Paul Tate is dead." "*Paul's dead.*" Nothing sounded right—they were sentences from an alien, out-of-this-world language. Words which, until that day, I had never imagined could exist together.

Right outside the door was a flower stand, and for an instant I wondered whether I should buy some for India. The vendor saw me looking and enthusiastically said the roses were especially nice today. The image of those red flowers brought me around fast and sent me dashing down the street in search of a cab.

The driver had on a monstrous black-and-yellow-plaid

golf cap with a fuzzy black pompon on it. It was so bad-looking that I had a desperate urge to knock it off his head and say, "How can you wear that when my friend just died?" There was a miniature soccer ball hanging by a string from the rearview mirror. I kept my eyes shut for the rest of the trip so I wouldn't have to see these things.

"Wiedersehen!" he chirped over his shoulder, and the cab pulled away from the curb. I turned to face their building. It looked new and had the familiar plaque on the wall saying the original building that had been there was destroyed in the war. This one had been put up in the 1950s.

I pressed the button in the call box and was disconcerted by how quickly her answer came. I wondered if she had been sitting by the buzzer since our phone conversation.

"Joe, is that you?"

"Yes, India. Before I come up, would you like me to go to the store or anything for you? You want some wine?"

"No, come up."

Their apartment was freezing cold, but she stood in the doorway wearing my favorite yellow T-shirt and a white linen skirt that looked as if it should have been worn in the dog days of August. Her feet were bare, too. Both the Tates seemed completely oblivious to the cold. I gave up being bewildered once I realized it made total sense in a way: both of them had so much bubbling, steaming life-energy that some of it inevitably ended up being turned into thermal units. This thought made so much sense to me that I had to test it out. Once, when we were waiting for a tram on a mean, godawful, cold, foggy night in October, I "accidentally" touched Paul's hand. It was as warm as a coffeepot. But that was all over now.

Their apartment was ominously clean. I guess I half expected it to be turned upside down for some reason, but it wasn't. Magazines were carefully fanned out across the bamboo coffee table, silk pillows upright and undented on the couch . . . The worst thing of all was that their table was still set for two. Everything—place mats, wineglasses, silverware. It gave the illusion that dinner was due to arrive at any moment.

"Do you want a cup of coffee, Joe? I just made a pot."

I didn't, but it was easy to see she wanted to be up and moving, doing something with her hands and body.

"Yes, that'd be great."

She brought out a tray jammed with big coffee mugs, a heavy porcelain sugar and cream set, a plate of sliced pound cake, and two linen napkins. She fooled around with the coffee and cake as long as she could, but finally her spring ran down and she was still.

Her empty hands began to fiddle and crawl up and over each other, while at the same time she tried to give me a comfortable, uncomplicated smile. I put the warm mug down and rubbed my mouth with my fingers.

"I'm a widow, Joe. A *widow*. What a fucking strange word."

"Will you tell me what happened? Can you?"

"Yes." She took a deep breath and closed her eyes. "He always does his exercises—those exercises before dinner. He said they relaxed him and made him hungry. I was in the kitchen making—" She threw her head back and groaned. Covering her face with her hands, she slid off the couch and onto the floor. Curled into a fetal position, she wept and wept until there was nothing left. When I thought she was done, I slipped down beside her and put my hand on her back. The touch started her off again, and she crawled, still crying, into my lap. It was a long time before silence returned.

He had been doing sit-ups. They had a little joke where he always counted them off loudly so she could hear how good he was at them. She didn't pay attention when his voice stopped. She thought he was either tired or out of breath. When she came into the room he was lying on his back, hands clenched tightly over his upper chest. She thought he was kidding. She went to the table and arranged the silverware. From time to time she looked over at him, and when he didn't stop, she got mad. She told him to stop kidding around. When nothing changed she swept angrily around the table, preparing to tickle him into submission. She bent over him, fingers out and ready to attack. Then for the first time she saw that the very tip of his tongue stuck out from between his lips and there was blood around it.

The coffee tasted like cold acid in my mouth. She finished the story sitting at the other end of the couch, looking straight ahead at the wall.

"He had high blood pressure. A couple of years ago a doctor told him he should start exercising if he wanted to be safe." She turned to me, a hard metal line of smile on her lips. "You know what? The last time he went to a doctor they said his blood pressure was way down."

"India, did he tell you what happened at the Hilton that day?"

She nodded. "Little Boy?"

"Yes."

"You think his finding out about us did this to him?"

"I don't know, India."

"Me neither, Joe."

Paul was buried three days later in a small cemetery that fronted one of the vineyards in Heiligenstadt. He had discovered the place while on a Sunday walk and had made India promise that if he died in Vienna, she would try to have him buried there. He said he liked the view—ornate stone and cast-iron markers with a backdrop of hills and grapevines. Way at the top, Schloss Leopoldsberg and the green beginnings of the Wienerwald.

I knew some of the people at the service. A big bear of a man from Yugoslavia named Amir who loved to cook and who had the Tates over to dinner at least once a month. A few people from Paul's office, and a handsome black teacher from one of the international schools who pulled up in a bright-orange Porsche convertible. But I was surprised there weren't more. I kept looking at India to see if she was fully aware of the meager turnout. She wore no hat, and her hair blew light and free in the wind. Her face showed nothing but a kind of closed harmony. She later told me she was aware only of her grief and the last moments with her husband.

The weather was fine and sunny; for a few moments the sun cheerfully reflected off a polished gravestone nearby. Except for an occasional car and the crunch of gravel underfoot, it was quiet. A stillness you were hesitant to upset because, when you did, the glass around the moment might shatter and Paul Tate would truly and forever be gone, and we would soon be leaving him.

That's what I'd thought the two previous times I'd been to funerals—how you leave and "they" stay. Like someone seeing you off at the train. As it's pulling out of the station and you're waving goodbye to them from the window, inevitably they seem to diminish in size. Not only because you're moving and the physical distance is shrinking them, but because they're still there. You're bigger because you're off and away to something new, while they're shrinking because now they'll go home to the same lunches, television shows, dog, ink, and view from the living room window.

I turned from thoughts of Paul to how India was taking it. She was holding her purse to her chest and looking up at the sky. What did she see there? I wondered if she was looking for heaven. Then she closed her eyes and lowered her head slowly. She hadn't cried at all that day, but how long could she hold out? I took a step toward her; she must have heard my feet on the gravel, because she turned and looked at me. Simultaneously, two very strange things happened. First, instead of seeming on the verge of tears or some kind of violent emotion, she looked, well, *bored.* That in itself was disconcerting, but then, an instant later, her face broke into a glorious smile, the kind that comes only when something wonderful happens to you for no reason at all. It was good I didn't have to say anything, because I would have been speechless.

The minister from the English church finished his "ashes-to-ashes" litany. I had no idea what connection he had to the Tates. He evidently hadn't known Paul, because he spoke in a professionally sympathetic voice that had neither warmth nor sadness in it. The interesting thing to me was that he had the same name as the priest in my hometown—the man who'd delivered the funeral services for both Ross and my mother.

When everything was done, I waited while the people said their last words to India. She looked fine; once again I had to admire how strong and sure she was, notwithstanding the smile of a few minutes before. She was not the kind of woman who would self-indulgently fall into her sadness and never re-emerge. Death was forever and horrible, but its force didn't own her as it did so many others in the same situation. I knew the difference, too, because I had seen Ross's death drown my mother in its undertow. Now, watching India walk toward me, I could see that would never happen to her.

"Take me home, Joe?" The wind gusted, and a drift of her hair blew across her face. Although I had expected her to ask, I still felt touched and honored that she wanted me with her then. I took her arm, and she pulled it tight to her side. For a moment I felt the curve and hardness of one of her ribs on the back of my hand.

"I thought it was an okay service. Didn't you? At least it was harmless."

"Yes, you're right. I think those Diane Wakoski poems were lovely."

"Yeah, well, she was Paul's favorite."

The Yugoslav passed and asked if we wanted a ride into town. India said thanks but she wanted to walk for a while, we'd catch the tram a few blocks away. I'd assumed she'd want to go by cab, but I said nothing. When he was gone, we were the only ones left in the cemetery.

"Do you know how they bury people in Vienna, Joe?" She stopped on the gravel path and turned so she was looking down one of the short, orderly rows of grave markers.

"How do you mean?"

"It's not like in America, see? I'm a big expert on it now. Ask me anything. In the States you buy yourself a little plot of ground—your very own piece, right?—and it's yours forevermore. Not here, baby. You know what happens in merry old Wien? You *rent* a place for ten years. That's right, no kidding! You rent a plot in the cemetery for ten years, and then you have to pay on it again when the time's up or else they'll exhume you. Dig you right back up. One of the guys here told me some graveyards are so popular that even if you keep making your rent payments, they still dig you up after about forty years so someone *else* can rest in peace for a while. Oh, shit!"

I looked at her; she looked sick and tired of the world. I squeezed her arm and accidentally bumped into the softness of her breast. She didn't seem to notice.

"I know what I'll do, Joe." She started crying and wouldn't look at me. Staring straight ahead, she kept walking. "After ten years here, you and I will get Paul and we'll move him to a brand-new graveyard! A new place in the sun. Maybe we'll get a mobile home and have it fitted out for him. Move him around all the time. He'll be the best-traveled body in town." She shook her head; the tears flew away from her face. The only sounds in the world were her high heels hitting the pavement and the short gasps for breath.

All the way home on the tram she held my hand tightly

and looked at the floor. The crying had flushed her face, but it had begun to pale again by the time we reached her stop. I tugged gently on her arm. For the first time she looked from the floor to me.

"Are we here? Would you mind sticking around, Joe? Do you mind coming home with me for a while?"

"*Selbstverständlich.*"

"Joey, I hate to tell you this, but you speak German like Colonel Klink on *Hogan's Heroes.*"

"Oh, yeah?"

"Yeah. Come on, let's get out of here."

The tram glided to a stop. We descended the steep metal steps to the street. I took her arm again, and she pulled it to her side. I remembered the time I'd watched the Tates walk away from me at the Café Landtmann. She had held Paul's arm that way, too.

"How did you feel after your brother's death?"

I swallowed and bit my lip. "Do you want to know the truth?"

She stopped and drilled me with one of her looks. "Will you tell me the truth?"

"Of course, India. How did I feel? Good and bad. Bad because he was gone and because he had been so much a part of my life up to that point. Big brothers really are important to you when you're young."

"I believe you. So where did you get off feeling good? Where did that come from?"

"Because kids are omnivorous in their greed. You said so yourself, remember? Yes, I was sorry he was gone, but now I could have his room and his desk, his football and the Albanian flag I'd always coveted."

"Were you really like that? I don't believe it. I thought you said you were such a good little kid."

"India, I don't think I was any different from most boys or girls that age. Ross had been bad for so long that he owned almost all of my parents' attention. Now all of a sudden I was about to get that attention. It's terrible to say, but you said you wanted to hear the truth."

"Do you think it was bad to feel that way?"

We reached the door to her building, and she went digging around in her pocketbook for her keys. I ran my hand lightly down the row of plastic buzzers.

"Was I bad? Sure, I was a nasty little rat. But I think that's the way most kids are. People are so indifferent to them so much of the time, *because* they're kids, they just naturally grab for whatever they can get. People pay attention to children the way they do to dogs—once in a while they kiss and hug and smother them with a thousand presents, but it's all over in two seconds, and then the grownups want them out of there."

"Don't you think parents love their kids?" She turned the key in the lock and pushed the heavy glass door open.

"If I were to generalize, I'd say they love them but wish they'd stay at a good distance. Once in a while they want them around so they can giggle and laugh and have fun with them, but never for very long."

"Seems as if all you're saying is kids are dull."

"Yes, India, I'd agree to that."

"Were you a dull kid?" She turned to me and dropped the keys into her purse in one movement.

"Compared to my brother I was. I was dull and good. Ross was interesting and bad. But really bad. Even evil sometimes."

She reached over and took a thread off my coat. "Maybe that's why your parents paid more attention to him than to you."

"Because he was a bad boy?"

"No, because you were dull."

The stairwell was damp and dark after our having been outside in the sun for so long. I decided to say nothing to India's mean remark. She went ahead of me. I watched her legs climb the stairs. They were so nice.

The apartment was a mess. It was the first time I'd been back there since the day Paul died. Cardboard boxes on the floor, the couch, and the windowsill. Men's clothes and shoes unceremoniously dumped into them; some were already brimming over with socks, ties, and underwear. Over in a corner three boxes were sealed with shiny brown tape and stacked out of the way. There was no writing on any of them.

"Are these Paul's things?"

"Yes. Doesn't it look as if we're in the midst of a fire sale? I got so uncomfortable opening closets and drawers and seeing his things everywhere I decided to lump it all together and give it away."

She walked into the bedroom and closed the door. I sat down on the edge of the couch and shyly peered into an open box on the floor near my foot. I recognized a green sport shirt Paul had often worn. It was ironed and, unlike the other clothes in there, folded neatly and placed on top of some brown tweed pants I'd never seen before. I reached into the box and, after a quick glance at their bedroom door, took the shirt out and ran my hands across it. I looked at the door again and brought the shirt up to my nose to smell. There was nothing—no Paul Tate left in it after its washing. I put it back and unthinkingly brushed my hands off on my pants.

"I'll be out in a minute, Joe!"

"Take your time. I'm fine out here."

I was about to get up and look in some of the other boxes when I heard the door open. She stuck her head out, and I caught a second's flash of black underwear before I met her eyes.

"Joe, would you mind waiting a little longer? I feel all dirty and gritty from this morning and I'd like to take a quick shower. Is that okay?"

A picture of her standing naked in the shower, shining wet, made me hesitate before I answered. "Sure, of course. Go ahead."

I thought of the film *Summer of '42,* where the beautiful young woman seduces the boy after she's learned her husband has been killed in the war. I heard the first spit of the shower and felt a full erection growing thick and randy down the inside of my thigh. It made me feel perverse and guilty.

I stepped over to a smaller box filled with all sorts of letters and bills, an empty green checkbook, and a number of fountain pens. I picked up a handful. Paul would only use fountain pens, and holding them, I realized I wanted one as a keepsake—don't ask me why. Then a strange thing happened: I was afraid if I asked India she would say no, so I decided to just take one and say nothing about it. I'm not really a thief by nature, but this time I did it without hesitation. There was a fat black and gold one. It looked old and sedate, and on the cap it said *Montblanc Meisterstück No. 149.* There were two others like it in the box, so I assumed that even if India was planning on keeping them she'd never miss this one. I slid it into my pocket and walked over to the window.

The shower stopped, and I listened carefully to the small distant sounds that followed. I tried to imagine what India was doing: toweling her hair dry or dusting powder onto her arms, her shoulders, her breasts.

A woman in a window across the courtyard saw me and waved. I waved back; she waved again. I wondered if she thought I was Paul. What a chilling, uneasy thought. She kept waving slowly like a sea fan under water. I didn't know what to do, so I turned around and went back to the couch.

"Joe, I thought of what I want to do."

"Okay."

"You're going to hate it."

I looked at the closed door and wondered if she could do anything I would hate.

She came out of the bedroom a few minutes later wearing a hooded gray sweatshirt, old Levi's, and a pair of sneakers.

She wanted to go jogging down by the river. She said I
didn't have to go with her unless I wanted to—she felt better now. She wanted to "clean a few miles" out of her sys-
tem. It made perfect sense, and I told her I'd go to keep her
company. We walked from their place down to the path beside the Danube Canal, which was long and straight and
perfect for running. I had a book with me, and I sat down on
a wooden bench while she padded off. There were scattered
mobs of seagulls diving and floating over the fast-flowing
water. A few old men were fishing from the banks; once in a
while a couple with a baby carriage walked slowly past. All
of us were playing hooky from the day.

I knew India would probably be gone for at least half an
hour, so I looked at the water and wondered what was going
to happen now. How long would she remain in Vienna? If
she left, would she want me to go with her? Would I want
to go with her?

Until I'd met the Tates I'd been so comfortable here. I
didn't know exactly how happy I was, but by the time I had
adjusted my rhythm and pace to that of the city, I fully realized how lucky I was to have that.

In a couple of months what would she want to do?
Where would she want to go? As appealing as she was, India
was a restless woman, and her sense of wonder needed constant refueling from new stimuli for her to be happy. What
if she wanted me with her, but in Morocco or Milan?
Would I go? Would I pack up my life and move it at her
whim?

I chided myself for being so sure of things. Also, the way I
had already dismissed Paul from both our lives was obscene.

I reached into my pocket and brought out his fountain
pen. I held it up in front of me. If I'd dusted it for finger-
prints, his would be on it somewhere. All of his left thumb
perhaps, or the right-hand pinkie. I held it up to the paling
sun and saw ink in it. Ink *he'd* put in. Dear Paul— A few
days after you fill this pen you'll be dead. I undid the cap

and frowned at the ornately engraved gold and silver point. How old was this thing? Had I stupidly taken an antique that was worth a fortune? I knew nothing about pens. Guiltily I screwed the cap back on and closed my hand over it, hiding it from the world.

The tapping of India's sneakers came up on one side; I had just enough time to put the pen away before she was there. Her face was flushed, and she was breathing hard through her mouth. I turned to meet her and was surprised when she came right up to me and put both hands on my shoulders.

"How long was that?"

I looked at my watch and told her twenty-three minutes.

"Good. I don't feel any better, but at least I'm exhausted now, and that helps."

She looked at the sky, putting her hands on her hips. She walked off a little and stood panting. "Joey? I know we're probably thinking about the same things now, right? But could we please not talk about anything for a while at least?"

"India, there's no hurry."

"I know, and you know, but tell the little gremlin inside me who keeps saying I've got to get everything together now and settled *now* so I can start right in on a new life. Tell him that. It's ridiculous, isn't it?"

"Yes."

"I know. I'm going to try and ignore it the best I can. Hey, why should I care if things are settled? What am I, crazy? My husband just died! Here I am, trying to make everything right again on the same day they buried him!"

She turned halfway around and ran one hand through her hair. I felt totally helpless.

7

After it snows in the mountains, the roads are in charge. There is nothing you can do about this but follow their whim. You drive slowly and hope the next turn will be friendly—that the trucks will already have passed through and there will be gravel spread over the surface like cinnamon or chocolate sprinkles on a cone. But this is wishful thinking; too often the snow glistens and is packed tight—it's been waiting for you in its nastiest mood. The car begins to slip and drift in a slow dream of danger.

Although I was trying to drive well and carefully, I was petrified. India had been giggling only a moment before.

"What are you laughing at?"

"I like this, Joey. I like driving on these roads with you."

"What? This stuff is dangerous as hell!"

"I know, but I like that, too. I like it when we whish back and forth."

"Whish, huh?" I turned and looked at her as if she was nuts. She laughed.

We were twenty kilometers from our *gasthaus*, and the sun that had been so bright and friendly that morning when we'd gone out for the drive had dropped behind the mountains. It had taken its yellow cheer with it, and in a moment things everywhere were a sudden, melancholy blue.

What if we broke down out here? The last person we'd seen was a child standing with a sled by the side of the road. He stared stupidly at us as if he'd never seen a car before. He probably hadn't. They probably didn't have cars this far out in the hinterlands.

She reached over and squeezed my knee. "Are you really all that worried?"

"No, of course not. I just don't know where we are, and

I'm hungry, and these damned roads give me the willies."

Still smiling, she stretched luxuriously and yawned.

We passed a road sign that said BIMPLITZ—4 KILOME-
TERS. It looked tiny against the backdrop of the mountains.
I silently wished we were staying in Bimplitz, no matter how
ghastly it was.

"Did I ever tell you about the time we saw the bear in Yugoslavia?"

Something quieted in me for the first time in minutes. I
loved India's stories.

"Paul and I were driving way off in the country somewhere. Just driving around. Anyway, we came over this
rise, and out of nowhere this goddamned *bear* loomed up
in the middle of the road. At first I thought it was some
crazy guy in a gorilla suit or something, but it was a bear
all right."

"What did Paul do?" We passed through Bimplitz and it
was ghastly all right.

"Oh, he loved it. Slammed on the brakes and pulled up
next to it as if he were going to ask for directions."

"What'd he think it was, a safari park?"

"I don't know. You know what Paul was like. Stanley and
Livingstone personified."

"What happened?"

"So he pulled up next to it, but by then these two guys
had appeared out of nowhere and were standing next to the
thing. One of them was holding a big thick chain that was
attached to a brass ring through the bear's nose. Both guys
started screaming out, 'Pho-to! Pho-to!' and the bear did a
little dance."

"That's what they were there for? They stopped cars so
you could take a picture of yourself with their bear?"

"Sure, that's how they made their living. The problem
was, they were out there in the middle of cloud-cuckooland,
and I don't know how many cars went down that road every
day, much less tourists."

I knew the answer to my next question, but I asked anyway. "Did Paul do it?"

"Do it? He *loved* it! Didn't you ever see the picture on the living room wall? He showed it to everybody fifteen times. Mr. Big Game Hunter. Frank Buck."

Why did India like me? The stories she told about her dead husband made him sound like the perfect companion—witty, adventurous, thoughtful, loving. If I had seen a bear in the road I would have run all the way home. The five o'clock blues seeped through my pores; even her presence didn't help.

"Look, Joey, that's the name of our town, isn't it? It's only ten kilometers."

The car did another squiggle on the ice, but seeing the sign made me feel a little better. Maybe the owners of the *gasthaus* would lend me a gun so I could go out and shoot myself before dinner. I reached over and turned on the radio. A disco tune leaped out of the dashboard, strange and out of place in these surroundings. India turned it up and started singing along. She knew every word.

> "Do just what you have to do,
> but don't tell me no lie.
> Soon the time is here again,
> Sundays in the sky."

It was a good song that made you want to hop around and dance, but I was surprised she knew every verse. She was still humming the tune when we arrived.

Our *gasthaus* was set back from the road and up a small hill, which the car gladly climbed, knowing its job was over for the day. I got out and stretched out of my neck the tension cramps that had been gathering all afternoon. The air was silent and full of the smell of woodsmoke and pine. Standing there, waiting for India to gather her things from the back seat, I looked at the mountains that swept the horizon. I was filled with a contentment that brought tears to my eyes. It had been a long time since I had felt that way. The night we'd be spending together smiled at me with white teeth and diamonds in its hands. We would go up to a room with white-and-red-flowered curtains, wood floors that rose and fell under your bare feet as you crossed to the bed, and a small green balcony that made you stand close together if you wanted to be out there at the same time. I had been to the place by myself several times and had vowed to take India there when the snows came and the area was at its most beautiful.

"Joey, don't forget the radio."

Her arms were full of coats and her hiking boots. She smiled so knowingly I almost thought she'd read my mind.

We walked up to the *gasthaus*; the clack of her wooden clogs on hard ground was the only sound.

An attractive woman in a loden and velvet suit was behind the reception desk and seemed genuinely glad to see us. Without thinking, I signed us in as Joseph and India Lennox. There was a section on the registration form that asked for our ages, but I left it blank. India was looking over my shoulder as I put the pen down. She gave me a nudge and told me to fill that part in, too.

"Just write at the bottom you like older women."

She walked up the wide wooden staircase. I followed, watching her lovely body move from side to side in a comfortable slow sway.

The woman let us into our room and before leaving said dinner would be served in an hour.

"You done us good, Joe. I like it very much." She touched the curtains and opened one of the balcony doors. "Paul and I were once in Zermatt, but there were too many damned people around. I kept trying to see the Matterhorn, but some jerk was always blocking my view. What town did you say this was?"

"Edlach." I came up behind her. I kept my hands in my pockets, not knowing if she wanted to be touched.

Paul had been dead a month. In that time of pain and forced readjustment, I'd circled her warily and tried to be there if she needed me, gone when she gave even the slightest indication that she wanted to be alone. Often it was hard to tell how she was taking things, because she moved cautiously through that time, her volume turned way down, and a kind of dulled expression owned her face. We hadn't made love since Paul's death.

India folded her arms over her chest and leaned against the balcony railing.

"Do you know what today is, Joe?"

"No. Should I?"

"A month ago today Paul was buried."

I had a coin in my hand and realized I was squeezing it with all my might. "How do you feel?"

She turned to me; her cheeks were red. From the cold? Sadness?

"How do I feel? I feel as if I'm very glad we're here. I'm glad Joey brought me to the mountains."

"Are you really?"

"Yes, pal. Vienna was beginning to make me sad."

"Sad? How?"

"Oh, you know. Do I really have to explain?"

She put her hands on the balcony railing and looked out over the sweep of snow-covered land. "I'm still trying to put all my blocks back in their right places. Sometimes I pick one up and look at it as if I've never seen it before. It makes me nervous. Vienna is always reminding me of something else, of another block I can't find the hole for."

The dining room was decorated like a mountain hut. Enormous exposed beams, a floor-to-ceiling porcelain stove in one corner, and rough *Bauern* furniture that must have been around since the 1700s. The food was heavy, steaming, and good. Whenever we dined together I marveled at how much India ate. She had the appetite of a lumberjack. This time was no exception. Sad or not, she tucked into it with glee.

We finished with ice cream and coffee, then sat across the table from each other, both looking sheepishly at the exhausted battlefield of empty plates in front of us. Just as things were getting a little too quiet, I felt a bare foot going up my leg.

India looked at me, her face a castle of innocence. "What's the matter, bub, you nervous or something?"

"I'm not used to cuddling under the table."

"Who's cuddling? I'm giving you an extended knee rub. They've very therapeutic."

As she spoke, her foot kept moving up my leg. No one was in the room, and after a quick scan around, she slid down in her seat; her foot went higher. She looked me squarely in the eye the whole time.

"Are you trying to torture me?"

"Is this torture, Joey?"

"Extreme."

"Then let's go upstairs."

I looked at her as hard as I could, searching for truth behind her very naughty expression.

"India, are you sure?"

"Yup." She wiggled her toes.

"Tonight?"

"Joe, are you going to play Twenty Questions or are you going to take me up on my offer?"

I shrugged. She stood up and walked to the door. "Come when you're ready." She went out. I listened to her clog resolutely down the hall and up the stairs to our room.

Because I was alone in the restaurant, things became preternaturally still the moment she left. I looked at the empty

bottle of wine and wondered if I should fly to my feet or get
up slowly and *then* run up to the room.

I could hear all of the sounds coming from the kitchen:
the plink and clank of plates and silverware, a radio that had
been playing since we'd first sat down. As I got up to leave,
the song about Sundays in the sky that India had been ac-
companying earlier in the car came on the radio and I
stopped at the door to listen. It seemed a good portent of
things to come. When it ended this time, something clicked
in me: I knew it had just taken its place in my mind forever.
Whenever I heard it again, I would think of India and this
time together in the mountains.

When I opened the door to our room, it was a blast of
blazing white light after the darkness of the hall. India was
in bed with the covers pulled up to her chin. She had
opened both balcony doors and the place was an ice palace.

"Are we trying out for the Eskimo Pie team in here?
What's with the windows?"

"It's good, *pulcino*. Smell the air."

" 'Little chicken'? I didn't know you spoke Italian,
India."

"Ten and a half words."

"*Pulcino.* That's a nice nickname." I walked over to the
balcony and took a few deep breaths. She was right. It
smelled the way air should. When I turned to look at her,
she had her hands behind her head and was smiling at me.
Her arms were bare and soft peach in that sea of white
colors. They framed brown hair that flowed across the pillow in all directions.

"India, you look absolutely beautiful."

"Thank you, pal. I feel like a little queen."

With more courage than I usually had, I pulled the covers
down to see what she was wearing. She had on an old gray
sweatshirt of mine with the sleeves pulled up. It made me
feel even better: she had taken it out of my suitcase, and

that small but entirely intimate gesture told me she really was ready to begin our physical relationship again.

"I feel like a banana being unpeeled."

"Is that so bad?" I untied a shoelace.

"No—very tropical."

No matter how willing both of us were, I was still nervous; my hands trembled as I took off my clothes. To make matters worse, she watched my every move with a smile and half-closed Jeanne Moreau eyes. Try to be calm when you're playing to an audience like that.

Before I got into bed I wanted to close the window to shut off the arctic flow, but she asked that I leave it open for a little while longer, and I wasn't about to argue. She turned off the bedside lamp. I slid in beside her and took her in my arms. She smelled of clean clothes and the coffee from dinner.

We lay there unmoving, the cold air sweeping through the room like an icy hand searching for something in the dark, not necessarily us.

She put a warm palm on my stomach and began to move it slowly down.

"It's been a long time, pardner."

"I was beginning to forget what it felt like."

Her hand kept moving, but when I tried to turn to face her, she pushed gently with the hand to keep me from doing it. "Wait, Joey. I want this all slow."

Far, far away a train crawled across the night; in my mind I saw the staccato blur of its yellow lights and the matchstick heads at the windows.

I was about to grab her when her hand closed on my stomach like a pair of pliers. I jerked from the pain.

"Hey!"

"Joey! Oh, my God, the window!"

As I turned to look, I heard the sounds. *Clink-a-tank. Clink-a-tank.* Metal wings. Metal wings flapping slowly but loudly enough to fill the room with an evil tin racket.

"Joe, *Paul's* birds! His trick! Little Boy!"

The same toy blackbird Paul had used in his Little Boy trick that night at their house. But now there were three of them perched on the balcony railing. When the first slash of fear passed, I realized they were all facing us in a perfect row, their wings beating in sharp unison like tin soldiers on the march.

The room was blue-black, but somehow the birds glowed from within; every detail of their bodies was easy to see. There was no mistaking what they were and whom they belonged to.

"Oh, Paul, Paul, Paul—" India's chant was slow and sexual, as if she were peaking to some kind of horrific orgasm.

The birds leapt from their perch and flew into the room. They were suddenly ten times faster: giant houseflies careening through the kitchen window in the middle of the summer. They zagged and dropped, flapped in a madness of flight. *Bang, ka-chang, flank*—it sounded like some maniac throwing tin ashtrays at invisible targets.

"Stop them, Joe! Stop!" Her voice was low and hoarse, emptied by fear.

What could I do? What powers did she think I had?

I started to get out of bed, and from different parts of the room the three of them came at me at impossible speeds. I ducked and threw my hands up to protect my head. Their beaks cut into my arms, my back, one across my scalp. I struck out and hit one, but it did no good—there was just another deep gash on my forearm as a result.

Then it stopped. I looked up and saw they were once again on the balcony railing in perfect order, facing us. My hands were up near my face, a failed boxer ready to be hit again.

One by one they turned and flew back out into the night. When they were ten or fifteen feet away, they sparked into blue and orange and grass-green flames. Familiar flames—colors I'd seen before in Paul Tate's living room the night the real bird danced and screamed in its small burning agony.

Ross believed in ghosts, but I didn't. He even beat me up once after we'd gone to a horror movie because I refused to believe anyone could be scared to death by anything as dumb as ghosts. I did an article for a travel magazine in America on a haunted castle in Upper Austria, but it was rejected because the only thing I could say was I stayed up all night in the hauntedest room of all, reading, and never once heard a peep or growl from the previous tenants.

My father once told me having children was like discovering new and amazing rooms in a house you've lived in all your life. Without children you don't necessarily miss these rooms; but once they're there, your house (and world) becomes a different place. I think I could have somehow rationalized the night of the birds if it had been the only incident of its kind in my life, but after what happened the next day, I knew that my "house" had grown too, only in a terrible, unbelievable way.

On our way back to Vienna the next morning, India slept with her head against the window on the passenger's side. We had talked until daylight and then tried to sleep, but it was impossible. When I suggested we go back to town, she quickly agreed.

A few kilometers before the turn onto the Sudautobahn, I stopped at a traffic light in the middle of nowhere. The sides of the road were marble-patterned with snow and black earth, but the road itself was dry and flat. I was so tired I didn't realize the light had changed until I heard a car honk behind me. I moved forward, but not fast enough for him, because he flashed his lights at me to get going. I paid no attention, because Austrian drivers are silly and childish; if the guy wanted to pass that badly, he had all the room in the world. There were no cars coming from the opposite direction. But he kept flashing and that, combined with leftover fear and fatigue from the night before, made me want to get out and bust the fool in the jaw.

For the first time I looked in the rearview mirror to see who the hell it was and what kind of car they were driving. From behind the wheel of a white BMW, Paul tipped his black top hat. Seated beside and behind him were four other Pauls, all tipping their hats too and looking directly at me. My feet came wrenching off the clutch and brake pedals. The car jerked forward twice and stalled. India murmured in her sleep but didn't wake up. I kept looking in the mirror and watching as the other car pulled out from behind and moved forward. When it was alongside I looked, and all five Paul Tates, all five Little Boys, with their prim white gloves on, waved and smiled. All of them out for a Sunday drive. The BMW accelerated and was gone.

8

Hell will undoubtedly turn out to be a big waiting room full of old magazines and uncomfortable orange chairs. Plastic airport chairs. All of us will sit there, waiting for the door to open at the other end of the room and our names to be called out in a bored voice. We'll all know there is some kind of excruciating pain waiting for us on the other side of that door. The ultimate dentist's office.

We waited for Paul to do something more, but he didn't. We didn't see each other for a week, and our only communication was by phone once a day. Nothing happened, so I carefully suggested we try having coffee somewhere very public, very open, and very unintimate.

When India came into the restaurant she marched right over and kissed me on the forehead. I tried not to cringe.

"Joey, I got it figured out."

"What?"

"Why Paul's here, why he's come back." She swished her hand through her hair and smiled as if she owned the world.

"Do you love me, Joey?"

"What?"

"Just answer the question. Do you love me?"

"Huh, well, yes. Yes. Why?"

"Don't make it sound so passionate or I'll fall into a swoon. Hmmm. Mr. Lovebug. Anyway, Paul thinks you double-crossed him. We were all three great friends, right? Did everything together, all for one and all that stuff. It was okay because he trusted you and even asked you to take care of me when he went away. Trust, Joe. When he got around to discovering how we'd stepped all over that trust, it broke him in half. Snap!" She looked closely at me, then away. I could sense she was about to say something either hurtful or uncomfortable. "I think it *was* part of what killed him. There's no way to avoid it."

"Oh, India!" I feigned indignation, but I'd thought about the same thing a hundred times.

"Look, let's not start playing games with each other, okay? Paul died two days after your clinky scene in that men's room. Well, Joe, you should have seen what he was like those last two days before he died."

"Was he that bad?" It was my turn to look away.

"Yeah, it was bad. One night he started crying. I asked him what was the matter, and he tried to slough it off and everything, but, God, it was so completely obvious."

"India, how *did* he find out about us?"

"It's funny you've waited so long to ask." Her voice was all accusation.

"I was too embarrassed before. I was afraid you'd—"

"Forget it. The truth is, I told him. No, wait and hear me out before you say anything! I am the world's worst liar, Joe. I can never fib, because my face shows everything. Besides, Paul knew me better than anyone. You know that. He knew something was up the minute he got back from his trip, even though we hadn't gone to bed then. Will you stop looking at me like that, Joe? I'm telling you the truth.

"One time he asked if I wanted to make love. I said okay, but when we were ready he couldn't get hard. Not at all. That was no big deal, but when he knew it wasn't going to work, he blew up. All of a sudden he was asking me if I'd done it with you and if you were any good. All these shitty questions."

"Paul asked you if I was *good*?"

"You didn't know that side of him, Joe. He could be a totally mean son-of-a-bitch. The worst was, sometimes he'd really flip out and say these crazy, crazy things. Little Boy was Little Lulu compared to him then." She shook her head. "It doesn't matter anymore. The important thing is this time I've been telling you about. He kept at me and at me until I couldn't stand it. Like a little monster I ended up saying, Yes, yes, we'd done it all right." She stopped, closed her eyes, and took a deep breath. "And because I'm such a shit, I couldn't help throwing in that you were really good, too. Nice, huh? Nice woman."

I picked up a magazine and opened it to a spread on the Austrian actress Senta Berger. Senta on television, Senta with her children, Senta in the kitchen. "Senta's in the kitchen with Dinah, Senta's in the kitchen I know-o-o-o, Senta's in the kitch—"

"Shut up, Joe."

I dropped the magazine. "I feel as if my head is going to crack open. All right, India, so you told him about us. What is your idea now? Why *has* he come back?"

"You're mad, huh? Joe, he would have found out sooner or later—"

"I am not mad. I'm tired and scared and . . . scared. No, I realize you had to tell him. It's not that. Ever since he died I've known how much to blame I was. Partly to blame? Totally? Seven eighths? Who the hell knows.

"But the fact you and I slept together, India, had nothing to do with him. India, I *loved* Paul! I've never had a better friend in my life. I—" None of it was coming out the right way. I had to stop or else I would end up banging my head on the table in frustration.

She waited a beat, then ran her fingers down my cheek. "You mean you loved him and you loved me, but you ended up loving me different 'cause I'm a woman, right?"

"Yes, exactly." The words came out sounding so bleak and gray.

"Okay, but what you're saying only fits in with what I'm saying too. Listen to me carefully. Paul loved you too. He said it a million times, and I know he meant it. That's what hurt him all the more, see? He thinks you and I got together because you wanted to screw me and because I wasn't satisfied with him. That's all. Period."

"Part of that *is* true, India."

"Don't interrupt me. I've got it all straight in my mind and I don't want to get confused. Yes, part of that is true, Joe, but only part. We went to bed partly because we wanted each other, sure, but also because we just plain *like* each other; partly because we're good friends, partly because we're attracted . . . Do you see what I mean? Paul thinks we jumped at the first chance we had to get a little *fuck* in. As far as he's concerned, we stabbed him in the back after he'd been so willing to trust us. We were willing to throw all of that great love and friendship out the window just so long as we could get it off a few times. Understand?"

"Yes, but what's the point?"

"Joe, the point is, if we can somehow reach him and tell him, *show* him it happened because we love each other, then maybe he'll understand and not be so hurt and vengeful. Yes, it will still be bad in his mind, but put yourself in his place. You find your wife waltzing around with your best friend. Bang—you go crazy 'cause you think they're dumping everything good just for a few hours in the hay. But then somehow you find out—God forbid—it wasn't like that at all. Those two are *in love*. It would change everything, don't you see? You've still been betrayed and bitten, but there's not so much venom because it *wasn't* just sex, it was the real thing!"

"India, that would be a hundred times worse! Having sex is one thing—it's pleasant and great—but love? I would much rather hear my wife was having a fling than about to take off with my best friend because they're in love. Flings are emotional and temporary, they're all skin and senses. But love? With a fling she still loves you and everything will probably be okay again in a while, when she comes back down to earth. But there's so little *hope* when she's in love."

"That's true with most people, Joe, but not with Paul."

"What isn't true?"

"Joe, I was married to the man for more than ten years. I know this is how he's feeling now. You'll have to trust me. I know him, believe me. I *know* him."

"Yes, you *knew* him, India, but the man is dead. It's a whole new ball game."

"Oh, is he dead? I hadn't noticed. I'm so glad you told me."

While I fumed she ignored me and ordered a bowl of soup from a passing waiter.

"Please, India, I don't want to fight with you. Especially now. I just want to know how you can be so sure of things when it's all so bizarre."

"It's bizarre all right, but I'll tell you something. The way Paul's going about it isn't bizarre at all. It's my husband, Joe. I'd know his brand ten miles away."

I wanted to trust her judgment, but I couldn't, no matter how hard I tried. In the end I was right.

Whenever they were bored, Ross and Bobby played a game that inevitably drove me crazy.

"Hey, Ross?"

"Yeah?"

"I think we should tell Joe the seeeeecret!"

"The *secret?* Are you out of your mind, man? No one hears the secret. The secret is a seeeeeeecret!"

"You guys don't have any damned secret," I'd lisp, desperately hoping this time they would tell it to me. I was three quarters convinced there wasn't one, but I had to be sure, and they always knew when to nudge me when my belief was waning.

"Seeeecret!"

"The seeeeecret!"

"We got the secret and little Joe doesn't. You want me to tell it to you, Joe?"

"No! You guys are stupid."

"Stupid guys but not-so-stupid secret!"

This kind of bull-baiting went on endlessly until I would start either screaming or crying. Or if I was really in control of myself that day, I would walk regally out of the room to a chorus of *"seeeeeecret!"* behind me.

To this day I love to hear and be part-owner of any secret. It was easy to see India had attics full of them and that some of the most tantalizing had to do with Paul. But after the discussion in the restaurant she wouldn't say another word about why she was so sure of Paul's behavior. I constantly asked questions, but she wouldn't give an inch. She just *knew.*

Nor did she want us to have much contact until she had figured out the best way of reaching her husband. In the meantime, I went to all the English bookstores in Vienna and bought everything I could find on the occult. I made pages of notes and felt like a graduate student preparing for his doctoral thesis. Séances, Aleister Crowley, and Madame Blavatsky filled those days. *Meetings with Remarkable Men*, *Lo!*, and *The Tibetan Book of the Dead* filled my head. At times I felt as if I had entered a room full of strange and threatening people to whom I had to be nice in order to get what I needed.

It was a land of quacks and yowls, flying objects and great cruelty. I knew there were thousands of people "out there" who molded their lives around these things, and that alone gave me the chills.

Whenever I thought I had something interesting, I called India and told her what I had found. Once I burst out laughing in the middle of one of these conversations when I thought of how shocked any sane person who had been listening would be.

About the same time, I received a letter from my father. I hadn't heard from him in months. His letter was long and chatty and talked familiarly about his world. He still lived in the same town, although he had sold our old house and moved his new family to a modern apartment complex in the ritzy part of town over by the country club.

He is a calm and pleasant man, but his letters always betray a bit of the ace reporter hot for an exclusive scoop. For some reason he often talks in them about things like who's died or who's been arrested. These gory tidbits are inevitably prefaced by phrases like "I don't know if you remember . . ." or "Remember the girl who had all her teeth knocked out by her boyfriend? Judy Shea? Well . . ." and then his zinger follows—she eloped with a convict or put her child in a mailbox.

This one was no different.

Joe, I was going to tell you about this a long time ago, but you know me and how I forget to get around to things. Anyway, our old friend Bobby Hanley is dead.

I heard the whole thing, interestingly enough, on the radio. It was the first time I'd heard about him in years. I knew he'd been caught robbing a store a few years back and that they sent him off to prison for it. I guess he got out, because this time the dumbbell tried to kidnap some local girl. The police got wind of it and came. There was a big gun battle right up on Ashford Avenue by the hospital, if you can imagine that.

It happened last June, and I'm sorry I didn't tell you about it then. Not that it's the kind of news anyone wants to hear. It certainly is the end of something though, isn't it?

The letter went on, but I put it down. Bobby Hanley was dead. He had been dead for six months. Six months ago he was in a shootout, and I ... I was a million miles away about to meet the Tates. Ross and my mother, Bobby Hanley, and now Paul. Dead.

"Where do you want to eat dinner?"

"I don't care. How about the Brioni?"

"Fine."

The Vienna winter had come, announcing its arrival with thirty straight hours of sleety rain and fog that painted everything dark and coldly smooth.

I kept the windshield wipers on full tilt and drove slowly through slick streets. Neither of us said anything. I was eager to be in a warmly lit place, eating good food, safe for a while from everything out there.

Three or four blocks before the restaurant I turned down

a small side street. It was narrow; the buildings on either side were so high that a mountainous clump of fog hung down the length of it, trapped like a tired, lost cloud.

We were halfway through it when I hit the child. No forewarning. A soft, heartbreaking thud and a high scream only a child's voice could have made. In slow motion a small formless thing in a shiny yellow child's raincoat glided up and over the hood of the car. India screamed. Before it reached the windshield, the raincoat slid over the side of the hood and disappeared. India wept into her hands, and I put my head on the steering wheel, trying impossibly to fill my lungs with air.

"Get out, Joe! Get out and see if it's all right, for godsake!"

I did what I was told, but what did it have to do with me? Joseph Lennox hit a child? A yellow raincoat, a small hand crabbed in pain, another death?

It lay face down on the black street, all limbs and pointed hood splayed out, looking like an enormous starfish.

It made no sound, and without thinking, I reached down and gently turned it over. The hand fell off. I hardly noticed because I'd seen the face. The wood was split through one of the eyes, but the head remained whole. Whoever had carved it had done it quickly, indifferently. The kind of doll you often see for sale in stores, advertised wistfully as "primitive art." Pinned to the raincoat was a little note. It had been done in thick black kindergarten crayon. *Play with Little Boy, Joey.*

The waiter came and went three times before we were able to order. When the food came, neither of us made a move toward it. It looked magnificent—*vanillen Rostbraten mit Bratkartoffeln.* I think I ate one tomato from my salad and drank three straight *Viertels* of red wine.

"Joe, even before this happened I was thinking about what we should do. I came to a conclusion, and I want you to hear me out before you say anything.

"We both see that Paul isn't going to leave us alone. I don't know how much it will accomplish, but I think the best thing you could do now is go away for a while. I'll tell you why. Everything has happened so fast that I haven't been able to think straight for one minute. Either I'm scared or I'm turned on, or else I'm lonely for one of you, and I don't even know which one. Maybe if you go away for a month or two, Paul will come and talk to me. I know, I know, it's dangerous. It scares the hell out of me, but it has to happen sooner or later, or else we'll both go crazy, won't we? You and I can't begin to figure out our relationship until he lets us alone and stops these grisly stunts of his. I haven't told you, but he's done a few things to me when I was alone; they were *the* worst.

"Another thing is, if you do go away, we'll be able to think more clearly about what we want from each other and whether or not we really want to try and make this relationship work for us. I *think* I do, and you said you do too, but who knows now? The whole thing is distorted. Every day is so full of tornadoes; I can't see straight anymore. Can you?

"If you're gone for a couple of months, maybe when you come back Paul will have decided to go away. Or maybe we won't even want our relationship anymore ... I don't know."

I put my hands on my knees and looked down at my feet. Why did I wear such solemn shoes? One look at my feet told the world I was forever on my way to Sunday school. Who else wore black shoes every day of the year? I didn't even have a pair of scruffy sneakers in my closet at home; only another pair of black oxfords that were this pair's twin brother.

"Okay, India."

"Okay what?"

I looked at her and tried to hold down the tremor in my voice. "Okay-I-think-you're-right. I knew it was the only thing to do, too, but I've been afraid to recommend it. I was scared you'd think I was a coward. But there *isn't* anything I can do here, is there? Isn't it obvious? He despises me, and whatever I try to do is going to be futile." I was squeezing my hands together so hard it hurt. "I'd do anything for you, India. I'm scared to death now, but I would stay and help you fight forever if I thought it would do any good."

She nodded, and I could see she was crying. I left a few minutes later without having touched her goodbye.

PART THREE

The flight from Vienna to New York takes nine hours. As the plane took off I felt a profound rush of relief. I was free! Paul and India and death and anxiety—I was leaving it all behind.

That relief lasted all of about five minutes. What followed was guilt and a paralyzing disappointment with myself. What the hell was I doing running away? How could I leave India alone in the darkness? I knew then how great a coward I really was, because I didn't want to stay. If anything, I wanted to be in New York in an hour. A hundred thousand miles away from Vienna and the Tates. I knew it and hated myself for the joy that had slyly bloomed inside me when I knew I'd made it—I had escaped.

I watched the movie, ate all the meals and snacks; twenty minutes before we landed, I went to the toilet and threw up.

I called India from the airport, but there was no answer. I called again from the city bus terminal; the connection was so clear it sounded as if she were in the next room.

"India? It's Joe. Listen, I'm going to come back."

"Joe? Where are you?"

"New York."

"Don't be goofy. I'm fine, so don't worry. I've got the phone number there, and I'll call you if I need you."

"Yes, but *will* you?"

"Yes, Mr. Jet Lag, I will."

"You won't, India, I know you."

"Joe, please don't be a horse's ass. This call is costing you a fortune and it's not necessary. It's adorable you called and are concerned, but I'm fine. Okay? I'll write, and I'll really call if I need you. Be good and eat some cheesecake for me. *Ciao, pulcino.*" She hung up.

I smiled at her orneriness and her guts and my freedom. I couldn't help it. She'd ordered me to stay.

India hung on to a co-op studio apartment in the city on Seventy-second Street that had belonged to her mother. She had given me the key to it before I left. I went over and dropped off my bags. It was musty and dirty; but tired as I was, I gave the place a good scrubdown. It was night before I'd finished, and I barely had enough energy to stagger to the corner restaurant for a sandwich and a cup of coffee.

I sat at the counter and listened to the people speak English. I was so used to hearing German this language sounded bright and crisp as a new dollar bill.

I knew I should call my father and tell him I was in town, but I put it off so I could be by myself for a few days. I went to the bookstores and ate pastrami sandwiches and took in a few movies. I walked the streets like some rube from Patricia, Texas, gaping at the people and colors and life that floated in the air like an invasion of kites. Because I hadn't been there for so long I couldn't get enough of it. The weather was sour and cold, but that didn't stop me one bit. At times my head was so full of New York I actually forgot Vienna for a while, but then a sound or the way a woman touched her hair reminded me of India or Paul or something I knew back there.

I bought her a number of presents, but the one I liked
best was an antique rosewood box. When I brought it home
I put it on the dresser and wondered if I would ever give it to
her.

I got in touch with my father, and we set up a lunch date.
He wanted me to come up to the country to see their new
apartment, but I wiggled out of it by saying I'd come to the
States to camp out in the New York Public Library and had
to work my schedule around their hours. I could say that
sort of thing to him and get away with it because he loved
the fact I was a writer; anything having to do with "the
trade" was okay by him.

The real reason for my avoiding the visit was that I dis-
liked his new wife, who was irritatingly garrulous and suspicious of me. My father thought she was great, and they
seemed to have created a really happy life together, but
whenever I had appeared on the scene in the past, it had
thrown things out of kilter for all of us.

He liked pubs, so we met in front of O'Neal's on Seventy-second Street and Columbus. He caught me by surprise because he was dressed very nattily in an English
raincoat that made him look like an old James Bond. He had
also grown a whopping gray mustache that only added to his
flash. I loved him for this new image; when we greeted each
other with a bear hug, he was the one who let go first.

He was beaming and full of pep and said his new life was
going great guns. He's such an honest person that I knew
none of it was pretense or showing off. Good things were
happening to this man who for so long had his share of the
bad. What I adored about him was how he kept shaking his
head at all his new good fortune. If ever there was a person
who counted his blessings, it was my father.

We sat in a corner and ate jumbo hamburgers. He asked
me about Vienna and my work. I told him a few lies that
made it sound as if I had the world on a string. By the time
coffee was served, he'd brought out a bunch of recent pho-

tographs of his family and, handing them to me one by one, made little comments on each.

His wife's two children by a previous marriage had grown and were both on the brink of adolescence. My stepmother had begun to lose the nice figure she'd brought to their marriage, but at the same time, she looked both more relaxed and more sure of herself than when I'd last seen her.

There were pictures in front of their new apartment building, in the jazzy new living room, of a trip they'd all taken together to New York. In that one they stood in front of Radio City Music Hall looking shy and secretly frightened of what they'd gotten themselves into by coming.

My father handed them to me gently, almost as if the pictures were the actual people. When he spoke his voice was amused, but love had hollowed out a corner in it; it was plain he cared very much for these people.

I smiled at each and tried to listen carefully to his explanations, but after I've seen ten or fifteen of them, snapshots of people I am not intimately involved with make my eyes swim.

"This one, Joe, is of that birthday party we had back in October. Remember, I was telling you about it?"

I glanced at the picture and reared away from it as if it were on fire.

"What is this? Where'd you get it?"

"What, son? What's the matter?"

"This picture—what's going on in it?"

"It's Beverly's birthday. I told you."

Three people stood holding hands, facing the camera. They wore normal clothes, but each wore a black top hat—just like Paul Tate's.

"Jesus Christ, get it away from me! Take it away!"

People were staring, but none of them as intently as my father, the poor guy. I hadn't seen him for many months, and then this had to happen. I couldn't help it. I'd thought

Vienna was behind me and that for the time being I was safe. But what is safety? Physical? Mental?

When we were out on the street again, I tried feebly to make up a story about working too hard and needing a rest, but he didn't swallow it. He wanted me to come home with him, but I wouldn't.

"Then what *can* I do for you, Joe?"

"Nothing, Pop. Don't worry about me."

"Joe, you promised me when Ross died that you'd come to me if you were ever in bad shape and needed help. I think you're breaking your promise."

"Look, Pop, I'll call you, okay?" I touched his arm and started to move away. I knew I was going to start crying and I'd be damned if I'd let him see it.

"When? When will you call? *Joe?*"

"Soon, Pop! In a few days!" I hurried to the corner of Seventy-second Street. Once there, I turned back toward him and, sticking my arm up as high as it would go, waved. As if one of us were on a ship, sailing away from the other forever.

I didn't see them until I had already opened the door to my building. It was after midnight. The black man had pushed the woman into a corner of the entryway. He was slamming her head against the metal mailboxes.

"What the hell's going on? Hey!"

He turned; I could barely make out that the sides of his mouth were shiny-slick with blood.

"Fuck off, man!" He held her by the neck while he spat this at me over his shoulder.

"Oh, help me!"

He shoved her away and came at me. Without thinking, I kicked him as hard as I could in the crotch, an old trick I had learned from Bobby Hanley. The man gasped and fell to his knees, both hands clamped between his legs. I didn't know what to do then, but the woman did. Stumbling for the second, inner door, she flung it open with a bang. I followed, and it *whomped* shut behind us, locking. The elevator was there, we were in it before the man even looked up.

Her hand was shaking so badly she was barely able to press 7, the floor below mine. When the car started to move, she bent over and threw up. She kept retching even when there was nothing left. She tried to turn to the wall, but she started coughing and choking; I was afraid she couldn't breathe. I went over and slapped her hard on the back.

The doors slid open, and I helped her out of the elevator. We stood in the hall while she took quick, heavy breaths. I asked her for the number of her apartment. She handed me her purse and started down the hall. She stopped in front of a door, pointing. She started retching again, and without thinking, I took hold of her shoulders.

Her name was Karen Mack. The man had been waiting for her in the hallway and had punched her in the face the first thing. Then he tried to kiss her, and she bit him.

It came out gradually. I made her lie down on a bright-blue couch and wiped her face with a wet washcloth I'd been careful to soak in warm water. She didn't need any more shocks. The only liquor in the place was an unopened bottle of Japanese plum brandy. I opened it and made both of us take big, disgusting swigs. She didn't want me to call the police, but when I said I should go, she begged me to stay. She wouldn't let go of my arm.

The apartment must have cost a fortune, because among other things, it had a large balcony that looked out over hundreds of rooftops; it reminded me of Paris.

When I'd patted her hand enough and reassured her I'd stick around, she asked me to turn out the lights and sit next to her. The moon was full and lit the room with its own smooth blue light.

I sat on the thick carpet next to the couch and looked out at the winter night. I felt good and strong. Later, when she touched my shoulder and thanked me again in a low, sleepy voice, I felt like thanking her. For the first time in weeks I felt valuable again. A human being who had for once stepped out of his own selfishness to help another.

I woke up the next morning on the floor, but a heavy wool blanket was over me and one of the soft pillows from the couch was under my head. I looked toward the balcony; she was out there. She'd put on a robe and fixed her hair.

"Hello?"

She turned and smiled lopsidedly. One side of her mouth was swollen and purple, and I saw she'd been holding an ice pack to it.

"You're up." She came in and slid the glass door shut behind her. Although the balloon lip distorted her face, it appeared she had one of those incredible Irish-white complexions that go so well with deep green eyes, which she also happened to have. Big eyes. Great eyes. Her nose was small and nondescript, but strawberry-blond hair framed her narrow face and made it a wonderful one, in spite of the smudge-purple lip.

She took the ice pack away, and her tongue snuck out to give the spot a lick. She winced when she touched it. "How many rounds does it look like I boxed?"

"How are you? Are you all right?"

"Yes, thanks to you I'm all right. After you live in New York for a while, you stop thinkin' there are any heroes left, you know what I mean? You proved me wrong. What would you like for breakfast? And would you please tell me your proper name so I don't keep callin' you 'you.' "

"Joseph Lennox. Joe, if you like."

"No, I like Joseph more, if you don't mind. I've never

liked nicknames much. What can I give you for breakfast, Mr. Joseph?"

"Anything. Anything's fine."

"Well, from the looks of my icebox, anythin' can be a cantaloupe, or fresh waffles and Canadian bacon, coffee . . ."

"I would love waffles, Karen. I haven't had them in years."

"Good, you got 'em. If you'd like to take a shower, the bathroom's opposite the bedroom. Gee, I'm makin' it sound as if you've got all the time in the world. Can you stay for breakfast? I called the school and told them I was sick. Do you have to be somewhere? It's only eight o'clock."

"No, no, I've got nothing planned. Waffles and coffee sound like the best thing I could do this morning."

Her bathroom looked like World War III. Damp towels on the floor, hand wash hung limply on a clothesline strung across the bathtub; a twisted tube of toothpaste lay in the sink with no cap in sight. I worked my shower around her obstacle course and even cleaned up a little before I left.

The living room was a shock of sunlight and morning warmth; the dining table was full of good things to eat. The orange juice was in thick crystal goblets, and the silverware caught the fierce morning light and bounced it off the walls.

"Joseph, please come and eat before it gets cold. I'm a terrific cook. I made you seven hundred waffles, and you have to eat them all or you'll get a D."

"Are you a teacher?"

"Yes, indeed. Seventh-grade social studies." She made a wry face and flexed her muscles like a strongman in the circus.

She sat down at the table and picked up a fork. We both sat there and watched her hand shake. She slowly put it in her lap. "I'm sorry. Please, though, you go on and start eatin'. I'm sorry, but I'm still scared to death. It's sunny out, and it's over, and no one's goin' to get me now, but I'm scared. It's like havin' a bad chill, you know?"

"Karen, would you like it if I stayed with you today? I'd be glad to."

"Joseph, I would like that very very very *very* much. Which part of heaven did you say you came from?"

"Vienna."

"Vienna? That's where I was born!"

Vienna, Virginia. Her parents lived near there and raised greyhounds for dog racing. She said they were fine people who had both inherited so much money it confused them.

Karen went to Agnes Scott College in Georgia because her mother had gone there, but she hated everything except her history courses. Richard Hofstadter came to the college and gave a lecture on Jacksonian democracy. She was so overwhelmed by it that she instantly decided to transfer wherever he taught permanently, which turned out to be Columbia University in New York. Totally against her parents' wishes, she applied and was accepted at Barnard. Later she went on to get a master's degree in history at Columbia before she got tired of going to school. She liked New York so much that when she was finished she took a teaching job at a private girls' school in the lower sixties.

This all came out over the longest breakfast I'd ever eaten. I kept asking her questions so she wouldn't think about the night before. But you can eat only so many waffles. Staggering up from the table, I suggested through swollen cheeks that we go out for a walk. She agreed; it crossed my mind it would be nice to have a change of clothes, but I wasn't sure if I should leave her alone yet, so I went as I was.

The day was snappy cold, but it was clear for the first time since I'd arrived. West Seventy-second Street is a world in itself, and whatever you're looking for is usually there: cowboy boots, organic pasta, Japanese box kites . . . We promenaded up and down and spent a long time looking in store windows, comparing notes.

I fell in love with a pair of cowboy boots that she made me try on. I remembered Paul's story about the Austrians in the Vienna airport wearing them, but they were beautiful. I came close to buying them, until I found out they cost over a hundred and forty dollars.

We had lunch at a delicatessen. She had a hard time eating her corned beef sandwich because her lip was so sore, but she laughed and started purposely talking out of the corner of her mouth like Little Caesar.

"Awright now, Lennox. I told you enough about myself. What's the dope on you? You gonna open up or am I gonna have to pound it out of you? What's your story?"

"What would you like to hear?"

She looked at an imaginary wristwatch. "Your life story in one minute."

I told her a little about everything—Vienna, my writing, where I came from. When she listened, her eyes grew wide and excited. Without thinking, she touched me often when some part of my story moved or dismayed her. She said things like "No!" or "You've got to be kiddin'!" and I often found myself nodding to assure her that it was true.

An hour later we were having a glass of hot spiced wine at a glassed-in sidewalk café. We started talking about the theater; in a small voice I asked her if she had ever seen *The Voice of Our Shadow*.

"*Seen* it? Hoo, Joseph, I had to read that play for a drama class at Agnes Scott. I made the mistake of bringin' it home over vacation, and my daddy got hold of it. Wow! He picked it up and flew 'round the house like an eagle, yellin' about how they were makin' us young girls read books about juvenile delinquents and feelin' girls up! Hell, Joseph! I know all about *that* play!"

I changed the subject, but later, when I told her about my connection to the play, she smiled sadly and said it must be hard to be famous for something you didn't do.

The wine turned into a Cuban dinner and more talk. It had been a long time since I'd so comfortably shot the breeze and laughed and not worried about things. With India you quickly realized she expected you to speak well and interestingly because she was listening so carefully. A moment before you said anything, you were still shaping and polishing it so it would arrive in first-class condition. When I was around India, both before and after Paul died, every moment shook with such importance that I was sometimes afraid to move for fear I'd break something—the mood, the tone, whatever.

Here, on the other side of the world, Karen made you feel that with no effort at all you were the cleverest, wittiest devil in town and that laughter was meant to boom across a room and drain you of everything you had. Life wasn't easy, but it certainly could be fun. We made plans to see a movie together the next night.

We went to a revival of the original *Lost Horizon*. When we left the theater she was wiping her eyes with my handkerchief.

"I *hate* them, Joseph! All they have to do is throw me some violins and that old Ronald Colman and I'm a goner."

I wanted to take her arm, but I didn't. I looked at the sidewalk and felt glad she was there.

"I had this boyfriend a couple of months ago? He'd take me to movies like that and then get all mad when I started cryin'! Now, what did he expect me to do, take notes? New York intellectuals—ink for blood."

"Do you go with anyone special?"

"No, that fellow was my last big steady. Oh, you can go to parties. I even went to a singles' bar once, but I don't know, Joseph, who needs it? I get choosier the older I get. Is that a sign of senility? I go into one of those jittery places, and everybody's eyes are as big as TVs. It makes me all depressed."

"What was the name of your last steady?"

"Miles." She pronounced it "Molls." "He was a very big-time book editor. He gave *me* a rejection slip."

"Oh, yeah? Didn't he like your style?"

She looked at me and poked me in the ribs. Then she stopped dead in the middle of the sidewalk and put her hands on her hips. "Do you really want to know or are you just makin' chitchat?"

People walked by with smirks and expressions that said they knew we were fighting. I told her I wanted to know. Sticking her hands back in her coat pockets, she started walking again.

"Miles wore his watch when we made love. Do you believe it? Drove me completely crazy. Why would someone do that, Joseph?"

"Do what, wear a watch? I never thought about it."

"Never *thought*— Joseph! Don't start makin' me upset. I have great hopes for you. No man should wear a watch when he's makin' love. What is he—on a schedule? What would you do if a woman came into bed wearin' a big Timex on her arm? Huh?" She stopped again and gave me the big stare.

"Karen, are you serious?"

"You bet I'm serious! Miles wore this big hundred-pound dive-bomb thing. Every time. It'd end up cuttin' me to pieces. Then I'd lose all the bliss because it was tickin' away at me."

"Karen . . ."

"Don't look at me like that. You're lookin' just the way he did when I told him about it. Listen—a woman wants to be taken and ravished and adored by a man. She wants to forget the world and leap right the hell off the edge! But not here—tick, tick, tick—it is seven-oh-eight and thirty seconds. You see what I mean?"

" 'Taken and ravished and adored'?"

"That's right. Don't start embarrassin' me—you asked."

We went back to her apartment for a cup of coffee. It was raining again; I watched it smash against the balcony windows. The living room was a bright fortress against it. The blue couch, thick carpet, soft white drops of light in each corner. The great contrast was the pictures on the walls. I would have expected Bernard Buffet clowns or Picasso doves to go with the softness and exuberant colors, but it wasn't so. Behind the dining table was a sludgy brown Francis Bacon print in a dull silver frame. I couldn't make out much of what was happening in the picture except that the subject was melting. Otto Dix, Edward Hopper, and Edvard Munch rounded out the happy lineup.

When she came in with the coffee, I was looking at a big print of Munch's *The Shriek.*

"What's with all the gloomy pictures, Karen?"

"Aren't they scaly? Music to have nightmares by." She perched on the couch and, with the most delicate movements possible, arranged two places on the coffee table, complete with miniature place mats. It reminded me of the care little girls take when they set up tea parties for their dolls and stuffed animals.

"Miles said I was a secret psychotic. Me and my penny loafers and lemon-meringue blouses ... Miss Fair Isle Sweaters. Do you want sugar? Oh, Miles. Miles should have been a screenwriter for French movies. He needed one of those severe knee-length leather coats and a Gauloise cigarette hangin' from his lip in the middle of the rain. Here, Joseph, I hope you like your coffee strong. This is Italian and it's good."

I sat down next to her. "You still haven't explained why you like such melancholy pictures."

She even sipped gently. "You're hurtin' my feelin's, Joseph."

"What? How? What did I say?"

"You're *sayin'*, dear man, that I've got to like *this* kind of picture because I dress or talk *this* way. I'm not supposed to like anythin' black or sad or alone because ... Well, sir, how would you like it if I put you in that kind of little box?"

"I wouldn't. You're right."

"I know you wouldn't. You don't know me all that well yet, but you're pretendin' you do by sayin' things like that. How would you like it if I said, 'Oh, you're a writer! You must like pipes and Shakespeare and Irish setters. At your feet!' "

"Karen?"

"What?"

"You're right." I touched her elbow. She pulled it away.

"Don't do that! Stop tellin' me I'm right. Put up your dukes and fight." She made a bird-sized fist and stuck it up under my nose. The fun behind the gesture wrenched something loose inside me, and looking at her, I opened my mouth to say, "God, I like you," but she interrupted me.

"Joseph, I don't want you turnin' out to be a male chauvinist pig. I want you to be exactly what I think you are, which is very special. I'm not goin' to tell you about that yet, though, because it'll only give you a swelled head. First you saved me from that black dragon, and then you turned out to be nice and interestin'. I will be madder than hell if you end up disappointin' me. Understand?"

Her school was old and red brick; you felt wealth radiating out from it like heat. I stood on the other side of the street at three-thirty and waited for her to come out. She had no idea I'd be there. Surprise!

A bell clanged and girls' heads leapt up in every window. Voices and shouts and high laughter. Moments later they swelled out of the building in soft gray and white waves. Hefting books, looking at the sky, talking to each other; all of them wore gray blazers, matching gray skirts, and white blouses. I thought they looked wonderful.

I saw a blond woman who looked like Karen toting a big briefcase. I started blindly across the street, but saw halfway there that it wasn't her.

After half an hour she still hadn't shown, so I gave up and started home. I didn't understand it. At a corner phone booth I called; she answered on the first ring.

"Joseph, where are you? I'm bakin' a pecan pie."

I explained what had happened, and she giggled. "Today's the day I get out early. I went down to Soho to shop for our dinner. You *are* comin' to dinner, you know."

"Karen, I bought you a present." I looked at it clenched in my hand.

"It's about time you got me somethin'! No, I'm kiddin'. I'm very touched. Bring it along to dinner. I'll open it after."

I wanted to tell her what it was. It was heavy; the big Edward Hopper book with color plates she liked so much. I put it down on the small metal shelf beneath the telephone box.

"Joseph, tell me what it is. No, don't! I want to be surprised. Is it great?"

"Why don't you wait and see?"

"Stinker."

I wanted to put my hand through the receiver and stroke that smooth, velvet voice. I could see her face—the delight and the sauciness. I wished I was there. "Karen, can I come over now?"

"I wish you were here an hour ago."

I almost ran down the hall when I got out of the elevator. I arrived at her door with the book under my arm and my heart in my throat. There was a note taped up: *Don't get mad. We'll have the pie when I get back. Something came up. Its name is Miles and says it needs help bad. I don't want to go. Repeat—I do not want to go. I owe him for a lot though, so I'll go. But I'll be home as soon as I can. Don't be mad or I'll kill you. There's a good movie on the Late Movie. I'll knock three times. Don't be mad.*

I bought a pizza and brought it home so I could be there in case she got back early. She didn't. She didn't come back at all that night.

2

The next morning I got a letter from India. At first I looked at it as if it were a key or paper I'd lost long ago and, now that I'd found it, didn't know what to do with.

Dear Joe,
I know I've been rotten about writing, but please assume things have happened that kept me from it. There's been no real sign from Paul, although twice he's done little bad things to remind me he's still here. Since I know you'll worry if I don't tell you what I mean, the other morning I went to the kitchen and found a Little Boy glove on the table where he used to sit. As I said, small things, but I got scared enough and reacted like a maniac, so I guess he was satisfied.
I've made an appointment to see a famous medium here in town, and although I've never had much faith in those table thumpers, an awful lot of what I used to believe has been washed right down the drain in the last few months. I'll tell you if it turns up anything.
Now, don't take it the wrong way, but I'm enjoying living by myself. There are so many more

things you're responsible for—the things your other
half used to take care of without your even knowing
it. But the compensation is, you're free as a bird and
answerable to none. God knows, I liked living with
Paul, and maybe someday I'll like living with you,
but for now I like having the double bed to myself
and all options open.

How are you, slugger? Don't you dare misinterpret
anything I've said here, or else.

Little hugs, India

I swallowed my pride and called Karen's apartment. It
rang seven times before she answered. Each ring made my
heard beat faster and faster.

"Hello, Joseph?"

"Karen?"

"Joseph. Joseph, I'm so bad."

"Can I come down?"

"I spent the night with him."

"I sort of guessed that when you didn't show up for the
Late Movie."

"Do you really want to see me?"

"Yes, Karen, very much."

She was in a pink flannel bathrobe and ugly pink
bedroom slippers. She held the robe closed at the neck and
wouldn't meet my eyes. We went into the room and sat
down on the couch. She sat as far away from me as she
could get. The dead couldn't have been more silent than we
were for those first five minutes.

"Do you have someone over there in Vienna? Not any
here's or there's. Someone special?"

"Yes. Or maybe yes. I don't know."

"Are you lookin' forward to goin' back to her?" Her voice
took on the slightest edge.

"Karen, will you please look at me? If you're worried
about last night, it's all right. I mean it's *not* all right, but I
understand. Oh, shit, I can't even say that. I don't have any

right. Look, I hate the idea of your sleeping with someone else now. It's a compliment, okay? A compliment!"

"Do you hate me?"

"God, no! Everything is crazy in my head now. Last night I thought I was going to end up chewing the carpet, I was so jealous."

"You were?"

"Yes, I was."

"Do you love me, Joseph?"

"What a time to ask that! Yes, after what I felt last night, I guess I do."

"No, maybe you were just jealous. It's easy to be jealous, especially with somethin' like that."

"Karen, if I didn't care about you, I wouldn't give a damn about last night, would I? Listen, I got a letter from Vienna today, okay? I got a letter, and for the first time I had no desire to go back. None. I don't even want to *write* back. Doesn't that mean something?"

She was silent. She still wouldn't look at me.

"And what about you, anyway? Who do *you* love?"

She pulled one of the couch pillows into her lap and began smoothing it with her hand again and again. "You more than Miles."

"What does that mean?"

"It means last night taught me somethin', too."

We finally looked at each other over the miles of couch that separated us. I think we both yearned to touch but were afraid to move. She went on smoothing the pillow.

"Did you ever notice how differently people act on a Saturday afternoon?"

We were walking arm in arm down Third Avenue. It was noisy and wet all around us, but the sun was out. We tramped along, paying no attention to where we were going.

"What do you mean?" I reached over and fixed her green muffler. She looked like a bright bandit in the middle of a holdup when I was done adjusting it.

"Don't strangle me, Joseph. Well, if nothin' else, they all laugh differently. Kind of fuller. I guess maybe it's relaxin'. Hey, can I ask you a question?"

"Is it about last night?"

"No, it's about *her* in Vienna."

"Okay."

We crossed the street into a patch of sunlight. The street glistened; someone passed us talking feverishly to his friend about Alitalia Airlines. She took my arm and slid her hand into mine in my pocket. It was warm and thin, fragile as an egg.

I looked at her. She'd pulled the muffler down from her top lip. She stopped and pulled me against her with the hand she had in my pocket. "All right. What's her name?"

"India."

"India? What a nice name. India what?"

"Tate. Come on, let's walk."

"What does she look like, Joseph? Is she pretty?"

"She's a lot older than you, for one thing. But, yes, she's quite pretty. Tall and thin, dark hair, kind of long."

"But you think she's pretty?"

"Yes, but in a different way than you."

"How?" Her eyes were skeptical.

"India is fall and you're spring."

"Hmm."

Five minutes later, the sun snuck behind the clouds and stayed. The sky turned to steel, and people began walking with their heads hunched into their shoulders. Neither of us said anything, but I knew the day was failing, no matter how many truths had shown their faces along the way. There was love on both sides, but it was cloudy and formless. I felt that if I didn't do something right then, this cloudiness would drain the intimacy from the day and leave us confused and disappointed.

Ross and Bobby went to New York a lot. They explored the city as if they were looking for buried treasure and, in so doing, found just what they wanted. Manhattan is full of strange and mysterious places that hide under the city like a secret heartbeat: the windows over the front entrance to Grand Central Terminal that go up ten stories and look down over the inside of the building like God's eyeballs through dirty glasses. Or a bomb shelter on the East Side designed to hold a million people and dug so deep into the earth that a tractor moving across the floor looks, from one of the upper staircases, like a yellow matchbox with headlights.

The two of them collected these spots and told me about them once in a while. But they shared very little, whether it was cigarettes or a bottle of stolen liquor, and they were even more tight-fisted when it came to showing anyone these unknown, magical places.

Consequently, I almost swooned the day they offered to take me to the abandoned subway station off Park Avenue. It was the only one of their trove of places I ever actually saw with them. I decided on the spur of the moment to take Karen down there.

When we arrived at the spot on the sidewalk, I bent down and started to yank at one end of a long rectangular subway grate. She asked me what I was doing, but I was too busy groaning and pulling to answer. I realized after too long that there was a latch beneath the grate that had to be released before anything would happen. As soon as I'd done that, the thing flew right up and almost decapitated me. The two of us were down on our knees over a subway grate, huffing and puffing to get it up, and not a soul stopped or said a word to us. I doubt if anyone even looked at what we were doing. Welcome to New York.

A flight of steel steps went straight down into the darkness, but Karen climbed down without a question. The last I saw of her face, she had a little knowing smile on. I followed right on her heels and pulled the grate over me like a submarine hatch.

"Joseph, my dear, what the hell is this?"

"Keep going. If we're lucky you'll see a light in a minute. Follow it."

"My God! Where'd you ever find this place? Looks as if the last time a train stopped here was in 1920."

For some reason the station was still lit by two dim bulbs at either end of the platform. We stood there, and only after some time did the distant sound of a train break the enormous silence. It got louder and louder, and when it scrabbled through on an outside track, Karen put her arm around my shoulder and drew my head to hers so I would be able to hear her above the roar.

"You are completely *nuts!* I love this!"

"Do you love *me?*"

"YES!"

When we were out of there and had walked a few blocks, Karen suddenly grabbed my coat and swung me around to face her.

"Joseph, let's not sleep together for a while. I want you so much I'm dyin', I won't be able to breathe. Can you understand? It's goin' to happen, but let's wait until"—she shook her head from side to side in a delighted flurry—"until we're drivin' ourselves *crazy*. Okay?"

I slid my arms around her and, for the first time, pulled her close to me. "Okay, but when it gets to that point, it's *boom* and it happens. No questions asked, and either side gets to say boom. Fair enough?"

"Yes, fair enough."

She gave me an incredibly hard squeeze, which left me gasping. To look at her, you'd never have thought she was that strong. It made "boom" even more wonderful to anticipate.

I was in New York for almost two months before India called. I knew that, compared to my growing feelings for Karen, I had never truly been in love with India. I felt guilty about that, but Karen and New York and the excitement of this new life drew a thick velvet curtain between me and what had happened in Vienna. When I was alone I wondered what I *would* do if the call or letter came. I honestly didn't know.

When I was a boy the house next door to ours burned down. For a year after that I was terrified whenever I heard the fire alarm go off in town. It blew in such a way that you knew immediately where the fire was: five toots —western section, four—eastern . . . But that made no difference to me. No matter where I was, I would run for a telephone and call home to see if everything was all right. Finally, and it really was almost a year later, I was playing punchball after school when the alarm went off. No answering alarm echoed inside of me, and I knew I was all right again. *That night* the house on the other side of ours went up in flames.

"Joseph Lennox?"

"Yes?" I was alone in my apartment. Karen was at a faculty meeting. It was snowing outside. I watched it wisp and float as the connection went through.

"Vienna is calling. One moment, please."

"Joey? It's India. Joey, are you there?"

"Yes, India, I'm here! How are you?"

"Not so good, Joey. I think you have to come home."

*   *   *

Karen came in her front door with a big package under her arm.

"I see you lookin' at this box. Don't think it's for you 'cause it's not. I bought myself a little somethin' which I will show you in a minute."

I was always glad to see her. Neither of us had gotten to the "boom" stage yet, but for days both of us had reveled in the delicious edge the waiting created. She dropped her coat on the couch and bent down to kiss my nose—her favorite form of greeting. The cold steamed off her, and her cheeks were wet with melted snow. She didn't notice anything was wrong because she was in too much of a hurry to get on with her show.

I looked out the window and wondered briefly if it was snowing in Vienna. Paul had returned and so frightened India with his Little Boy tricks that over the phone she seemed on the verge of a breakdown. The curtains to their bedroom had burst into flame that night as she was getting into bed. It was over in a few seconds, but it was only the latest thing. She admitted that since I'd left he had constantly been at her, but she'd avoided telling me because she'd kept hoping he would come to her and talk. He hadn't, and now she was at the end of her taut rope.

"*TA-DA!*" Karen stumped into the living room in nothing but a Hawaiian print bikini and the pair of brown cowboy boots I'd admired so long ago in the shop window.

"You thought I'd forgotten, didn't you? Ha! Well, you old cayuse, I didn't. Happy Cowboy Boot Day. If I don't take these things off this minute, my feet are going to warp."

She sat down next to me and pulled them off. When she'd finished, she picked one up and ran her hand along its side. "The man in the store told me that if you take care of them with polish, this leather'll last you a hundred and fifty years."

She looked at me with a smile so loving and excited by what she'd done that for some seconds I thought, Fuck it, I cannot go away from this woman. I don't care about anything but this face and these cowboy boots and this room and this moment. That's all. Fuck it. What could I do in Vienna, anyway? What could I possibly accomplish there that India hadn't? Why did I have to go? Close that door in my mind, lock it tightly, throw the key as far away as I could. *Basta.* If I could keep my mind from opening it again or, better, forget that door completely, I would be home free. Was that so hard? What was more important—love or nightmares?

"You don't like them." She dropped the boot and pushed it a little with her bare foot.

"No, Karen, it's not that at all."

"They're the wrong color. You hate them."

"No, they're the best present anyone ever gave me."

"Then what's *wrong*? Why are you lookin' so sad?"

I got up from the couch and walked to the window. "I got a call from Vienna tonight."

Karen was unable to hide her emotions; the word "Vienna" made her catch her breath so sharply I could hear it clear across the room.

"All right. What did she say?"

I wanted to tell her! I wanted to sit beside her, take those lovely hands in mine, and tell her every bit of the story. Then I wanted to ask this wise and generous woman what in God's name I should do. But I didn't. Why involve her in this? It would be cruel and unnecessary. Whether I was right or wrong, for the first time in my life I realized love meant sharing the good and trying like hell to keep the bad away, no matter what shape or size. So I didn't say anything about the darkness in Vienna. I said only that India was in

very bad shape and had asked me to come back and help
her.

"Is she tellin' the truth, Joseph? And are you tellin' *me*
the truth?"

"Yes, Karen, both."

"Both." She picked up the cowboy boot again and placed
it gently on the coffee table. She put both hands up to her
ears as if suddenly there were too much noise in the room.
Strangely, the Munch print of *The Shriek* was directly behind her and she looked eerily like the bedeviled person in
the painting.

"It's not right, Joseph."

I went over to the couch and put my arm around her. She
came, unresisting. My mind was so blank that the only thing
going through it was how very cold her shoulders were. How
different from India, who was warm all the time.

"I want to say ten bitchy things all at once, but I'm not
goin' to, damn it. It's just not right."

I rocked her under my arm for a long time.

"I want to trust you, Joseph. I want you to tell me you're
just goin' back there to help that woman out, and as soon as
you can you'll come back to me. I want you to say that to
me, and I want to believe it."

"It's true. That's just what I was going to say." I said this
with my head resting on hers. She gave me a slight push
away and looked at me.

"Yes, you say it now, but I'm scared, Joseph. Miles said
it, too. Miles told me he just had to get some things straight
in his life and then he'd come back to me. Sure, sure. I was
such a sap. He didn't come back! When he left for his 'little
while,' he left, and that little while didn't end. I wanted to
trust him, too. I *did* trust him, Joseph, but he never came
back! That one time he called, right? You know what he
wanted? He wanted to get *laid*. That's all. He was sweet and
funny, but all he wanted was to get laid. Remember, I told

you I learned some stuff that night? Well, that's what." She started rocking again; only this time it was hard and mechanical, like a machine.

"I'm not Miles, Karen. I love you."

She stopped. "Yes, and I love you too, but who can I trust? Sometimes I feel so small and alone that it's like death. Yes, that's what death is—the place where you can't trust anybody. Joseph?"

"Yes?"

"I want to trust you. I want to believe every word you say to me, but I'm afraid. I'm afraid you'll say you've got to go for this little while and then . . . Aw shit, I *hate* it!"

She stood up and began walking around the room. "You see? You see? I'm so scared right now I've been lyin' to you! Even after that night with Miles, when I started realizin' things about my relationship with him, he called me. You didn't know that, did you?"

My heart dropped on hearing his name, but I kept quiet and waited for her to go on. It was some time before she did. She paced the room the whole time. Watching her small, bare feet cross the floor in the middle of that winter night made everything so much worse.

"He called me a couple of days ago, okay? I never have the guts to tell anyone just to stop, but with him I wanted to ever since that night. I mean, I wanted to ninety percent, but there *was* a little ten percent in there that kept sayin', Be careful, don't burn those bridges, dearie. You know what happened, though, the last time he called? This is the honest-to-God truth, too, Joseph, so help me. He called and wanted to take me ice skatin' at Rockefeller Center. He knows how I love to do that. Hadn't forgotten a thing, the skunk. Never misses a trick. A little hot cocoa afterward, too? But you know what I said to him, Joseph? Talk about burnin' your bridges? I said, 'Sorry, Miles, Karen's in love right now and can't come to the phone!' Then I hung up.

Me! I felt so good doin' it that I picked it up and hung up again."

She laughed to herself and, basking in the memory, put her hands on her hips and smiled at the wall.

"But you said he used you the last time you were together. Did you still want to go out with him after that?"

"Not at the time, no! I had you. But what about now, Joseph? You go away and he happens to call again. He probably will—he's got an ego as big as this room. What do I do when that happens?"

"If he calls again, you go out." I didn't want to say it, but I had to. I had to.

"You don't mean a word of that."

"No, I *mean* it, Karen. I hate it, but I swear I mean it."

"It wouldn't bother you?" Her eyes narrowed but said nothing I could understand. Her voice was ice.

"It would drive a stake through my heart, my love, if you want the truth-truth. But you'll have to. But don't lie to me either, Karen; there's a part of you that wants to, isn't there?"

She hesitated before answering. I appreciated the fact that she really thought for an instant before speaking.

"Yes and no, Joseph, but I think I've got to do it now. You have to go back to Vienna, and I have to see Miles again."

"Jesus Christ."

"Joseph, please tell me the truth."

"The truth? The truth about what, Karen?"

"About her. About India."

"The truth is, I hate the fact you'll be seeing him. I hate having to go back to Vienna. For a number of reasons I'm truly scared of what's going to happen when I get back there. I'm also afraid of what's going to happen here with you and him. Let's say I'm afraid of a lot of things now."

"Me too, Joseph."

3

I wore my cowboy boots the day I flew back. I felt funny in
them, the way they canted my whole body this way and that
like a drunken ride at an amusement park. But I'd be
damned if I'd take them off. I'd packed my bag the night
before; it was much fuller than when I'd arrived. My *life* was
fuller than when I'd arrived. But there was India and her
agony in Vienna, and a part of me, a new and, I hoped,
good part, said notwithstanding the near-happiness I'd recently found, my duty now was to return and do whatever I
could to help her, no matter how useless it seemed or how
much I wanted to stay with Karen in New York. Even
watching Karen that night, so small and defeated on the
couch, I knew that for once I had to sacrifice what I
wanted for someone else's well-being. Despite my pain
at having to leave America, the act itself might end up
being the only thing in my life that would make me feel a
little better about myself. What Karen had said was true
—it wasn't right, but it was necessary. Our parting was bad
and tearful. At the last moment we almost succumbed to it
by sleeping together for the first and only time. Luckily we
had enough strength of heart to avoid the mess *that* would
have created.

People think of Austria as a snowy, Winter Wonderland
sort of country; it is, except for Vienna, which rarely has
much snow in the winter. Yet the day I flew in, there was
such a bad blizzard that we were diverted to Linz and had to
take a train the rest of the way. It was snowing in Linz, too,
when we arrived, but it was a crisp, light snow and the flakes

came down lazily, at their leisure. Vienna was under attack. Winds made traffic lights jerk and twist on their cables. There were long lines of taxis at the train station, all of them wearing chains and covered with snow. My cabdriver couldn't get over the storm and spent the ride telling me about some poor man who'd been found frozen to death in his house, and how a roof collapsed at a movie theater under the weight of the snow . . . It all reminded me of one of my father's letters.

I was expecting a cold, dead apartment, but the instant I opened the door, the smells of spicy roast chicken and radiator heat surprised me completely.

"Hail the returning hero!"

India looked as if she'd come back from a month in Mauritius.

"You're so tan!"

"Yeah, I've discovered tanning studios. How do I look? Are you going to put your bags down or are you waiting for a tip?"

I put them down, and she came over and hugged me for dear life. I hugged back, but unlike the time with my father, I let go first.

"Let me look at you. Did you get mugged in New York? Talk to me! I've been waiting to hear your voice for two months—"

"India—"

"I was so afraid the snow was going to keep you away. I called the airport so many times they finally got me a private answering service. Say something, Joey. Did you have a million adventures? I want to hear about all of them right now." Everything came out in a machine-gun stutter. She'd barely catch her breath before the next sentence flashed out of her as if it were afraid it wouldn't get its chance before the next one came trampling through.

"—I decided to come over here and cook because—"

"India?"

"—and I knew . . . What, Joey? Is the Great Silent One going to say something?"

I put a hand on each of her shoulders and held her tight. "India, I'm back. I'm here. Take it easy, pal."

"What do you mean, take it easy?" She stopped with her mouth halfway open. She shivered as if the cold outside had pierced her. The basting brush she'd been holding in her hand fell to the floor. "Oh, Joe, I was so afraid you wouldn't come back."

"I'm here."

"Yes, you really are. Hello, *pulcino*."

"Hello, India."

We smiled, and she dropped her head to her chest. She shook it from side to side, and I gripped her more tightly.

"I'm *home*, India." I said it softly, a good night to a child you're tucking in.

"You're a good man, Joey. You didn't have to come back."

"Let's not talk about it. I'm here."

"Okay. How about some chicken?"

"I'm ready."

Our meal went well; by the time we'd finished, both of us were much happier. I told her about New York, but not about Karen. That was for some other time.

"Let me see how you look. Stand up."

She checked me out carefully, reminding me of someone looking over a used car before they bought it.

"You're not any fatter, God knows, but your face looks good. New York did you good, huh? How do I look? Like Judith Anderson with a tan, right?"

I sat down and picked up my wineglass. "You look . . . I don't know, India. You look the way I thought you would."

"And how's that?"

"Tired. Scared."

"Bad, huh?"

"Yeah, kind of bad."

"I thought the tan would hide me." She shoved back from the table and put her napkin over her head. It covered her eyes completely.

"India?"

"Don't bother me now. I'm crying."

"India, do you want to tell me about what's been happening or do you want to wait a while?" I pulled the napkin away and saw her eyes were wet.

"Why did I make you come back? What good will it do? I couldn't get Paul; I couldn't talk with him. He came and he came and he came, and each time there was a moment when I actually had the guts to say, 'Wait, Paul. Listen to me!' But it was so stupid. So *fucking* stupid."

I took her hand, and she squeezed mine in a scared vise.

"Everything is shit, Joe. He won't go away. He's having so goddamned much *fun*. What can I do? Joey, what am I going to do?"

I spoke as gently as I could. "What have you done so far?"

"Everything. Nothing. Gone to a palmist. A medium. Read books. Prayed." She brushed the air with her hand, dismissing it all with a contemptuous wave. "India Tate, ghost hunter."

"I don't know what to say to you."

"Say, 'India, here I am back with a million answers to every one of your questions.' Say, 'I'll kick out the ghosts and I'll warm up your bed again, and just ask me 'cause I'm your Answer Man.' " She looked at me sadly, knowing my answer even before I gave it.

"The sun is ninety-three million miles from the earth. The pitcher's mound is ninety feet from home plate. Carol Reed directed *The Third Man.* How are those for answers?"

She picked up a fork and tapped me on the back of the hand with it. "You're a jerk, Joe, but you're a nice jerk. Can I ask a favor?"

I'm not an intuitive person, but this time I knew what she was going to say before she said it. I was right.

"Can we go to bed?" As if she knew I'd hesitate, she didn't wait for an answer. Getting up from the table, she moved toward the bedroom door without looking at me. "Leave the lights on in here. I don't like to think of the house dark these days."

That last sentence struck me hard, and still not knowing what I'd do when I got there, I followed her.

On the plane I'd resolved not to sleep with India when I returned. A private promise to myself to remain true to Karen, however sophomoric that seemed. I felt that, if I kept that promise, somehow Karen would know or sense it in that profound and mysterious way women are capable of sensing things, and it would reassure her when we got back together again. I didn't know when that reunion would take place, but I was sure it would.

The familiar glow of the familiar lamp in that familiar room. India was taking two small brown combs out of her hair and had already unbuttoned the top brass button of her jeans. I could see the top line of white on her underpants. I stood in the doorway and tried not to watch or respond to the casual sensuality of her actions. For a moment, while her arms were raised high and angled over her head, she stopped and looked at me with a combination of desire and hope that made her look sixteen years old and open to everything in the world. How unfair! It wasn't right for her to show me this side of her when all I wanted to do was help, not love, her. I felt the pulse in my throat and was scared by the extravagance of my heart's response.

"You look as if you swallowed a clam shell. Are you all right?"

"Yes, but I have to go to the bathroom."

"Uh huh." She was already back into the private motions

of undressing and seemed to have barely heard me. I was grateful for that, because I needed time to break the uncertain spell she had cast.

I had only just clicked on the light in the toilet when she screamed.

The first thing I saw was her standing by the side of the bed in only her white panties, looking down. Her breasts were so much older than Karen's.

She had pulled the bedspread back. Laid carefully in a row were many centerfolds from *Playboy* magazine. The vaginas of the women had been cut out, and in their place were faces: old men, children, dogs ... All of them were smiling with the greatest glee. Written somewhere on each picture in big crude letters was WELCOME HOME, JOE! GOOD TO HAVE YOU BACK WITH US!

4

The Viennese, who are old hands at snow in the Austrian mountains, seemed dismayed that it had come to visit them in town, particularly in such abundance. Children and a few slow-moving cars owned the streets. While looking out the window, I saw both a man and his dog slip and fall down at the same time. Every few hours the snowplows tried to bully the snow out of the way, but it was useless.

India stayed with me that night, but I did no more than hold her in my arms and try to calm her. At her insistence I took the pictures off the bed and burned each to a gray-violet crisp in the sink before washing the ashes down the drain.

The next morning the sun shone weakly for a few hours, but by midmorning the sky had clouded over, and it was snowing hard again by the time we reached the street.

"I want to walk for a while. Can we walk?" She was holding my arm and watching where our feet went. With every step her high rubber boots disappeared up to the calf in the white.

"Sure, but I think it'd be better if we walked in the street."

"I don't know why, but I feel a lot better today. Maybe it's just being outside." She looked at me, and her eyes, straining to be happy and unconcerned, asked that I agree. The complete whiteness of the world did calm some of the violence of the night before. But I had a strong feeling that no matter what we did or where we went, we were being watched.

India reached down and took a handful of snow. She tried to pat it into a ball, but it was too fresh and light to stay together.

"Old snow is best for that."

We were standing in the middle of the street, and I kept looking around for cars. "India, are we going to walk or what?"

"I'm pretending this interests me so I can avoid asking why you didn't make love to me last night."

"Last night? Are you nuts?"

"I wanted you to."

"Even after all that?"

"*Because* of all that, Joey."

"But, India, he . . . he might've been there."

"Too bad. I wanted you."

"Come on. Let's walk."

She dropped the snow and looked at me. "You know what? You held me as if I were dying of the plague."

"Stop it!" My embarrassment turned to anger. The kind

of anger that comes when you know you're to blame but don't want to admit it.

"You said he might've been in the room. But you know what, Joe? He's been in the room for months. You know what it's like to have him there for months? It's shit, Joe. And, God, I wanted you back. If you came back, so what if he was there? Months, Joe. Live alone with him for months like this and then ask me why I wanted you last night. He's everywhere now; there's nowhere to hide. So take me and *let* him see us. I don't care."

What could I say? Better to explain it all, tell her about Karen, so at least she'd have a concrete answer? There are so many different ways to fail a person. Answer this question honestly, thereby hitting her again after she'd already been hit so many times? Keep quiet and add to the confusion, her valid fear that she was almost entirely alone now in the battle against her dead husband? Standing there, helpless, I felt the weight of her need, and I came close to hating her for it.

My heart was beating like an angry dog's, and I was so overdressed against the snow that I felt hot and bound in by all my clothes. If I'd had three wishes, I'd have rolled them into one and asked to be sitting in a Chock Full o'Nuts in New York, drinking coffee and eating doughnuts with Karen. That's what owned my mind then—coffee and doughnuts with Karen.

The year before he died, Ross had a girlfriend named Mary Poe. She was a tough babe who smoked two packs a day and had the longest fingernails I'd ever seen in my life. She'd been Bobby's girl for a while, but it hadn't worked out, and Ross'd inherited her. Between cigarettes, she laughed a lot and hung on Ross like tinsel on a Christmas tree. After they'd gone out for a few months, however, Ross grew tired of her and tried to end the relationship. It turned out to be one of the few times I ever saw my brother completely confused, because no matter what he did, she would not go away. He stopped calling her, wouldn't go near her at school, and for spite started dating her best friend. That didn't stop Mary. The crueler he got, the more she pursued him. She knitted him two sweaters and a pair of gloves (which he ceremoniously burned in front of her at school one day), called at least once a night, and sent him letters so drowned in Canoe cologne that our mailbox began to smell like a whore's handkerchief. At one particularly desperate point, he halfheartedly threatened to kill her, but she shrugged and said she was already dead without him. Luckily, in the end she found someone else, and Ross vowed he would never get involved with girls again.

Why I bring all this up is that I remember the scared, trapped look he used to get whenever the phone rang at night during that time. As India and I trudged down the silent, abandoned street that morning, I felt the same "no exit" way, only a hundred times worse because of Paul's immanence.

"Let's go in here for a coffee, Joe. My toes just went into shock."

It was midmorning, but because of the snow, the café was almost empty. A tired-looking old man sat with a glass of white wine in a corner, a chow dog asleep at his feet under the table.

We ordered, and the waiter, happy to have something to do, rushed behind the counter to get it.

Things were uncomfortably silent; I got so desperate for some kind of noise I was about to tell India a dumb joke, when the door opened and a big fat man came in with a dachshund right behind him. The chow took one look at them and leapt to attention, barking. The dachshund marched right over to the chow and nipped him on the leg. India gasped, but the big dog loved it. He jumped back and started hopping around, barking all the time. The dachshund took two steps forward and nipped him again. The two owners watched it all with big smiles on their faces.

India crossed her arms and shook her head. "What is this, the zoo?"

"I just noticed the dachshund's a girl."

India laughed. "That's the answer. Maybe if I bite Paul, he'll go away."

"Or at least he'll bark at you."

"Yeah." She stretched both arms over her head and, smiling, looked at me. "Joe, I'm being really stupid. I apologize. Maybe it's my way of paying you a compliment."

"How so?"

"Maybe I had so much faith in you I thought once you returned, everything would immediately be all right again, like I said last night, you know? Did you ever get that feeling about a person? That they can fix anything as soon as they get their hands on it? Yeah, that's what it was. I thought your return would send those bogeymen way the hell away."

"Bogey*man*."

"Yeah, singular. One at a time, huh? Let's go. This place is beginning to sound like *Born Free*."

The rest of the day went well as we roamed around town, relishing the feeling that the whole place belonged entirely to us and the snow. We went shopping in the First District, and she bought me a crazy-looking T-shirt at the Fiorucci store.

"When am I supposed to wear it?"

"Not when, Joe, *where*? It's the ugliest shirt I've seen since Paul's Hawaiian disaster." She said it as if he were only a step away, and I recalled for an instant all the good times we'd had together in the fall.

As time went on, I noticed how often both of us spoke of him in loving and nostalgic ways. India didn't want to talk about what he'd done to her while I was away in New York, but the days of Paul alive were always fresh and near to her, and I truly liked being swept back to the days of our joint happiness.

The snow held on for a few more days, and then one of

those weird, spectacularly warm and sunny spells came and erased most traces of winter. I'm probably one of the few people who don't like that kind of weather. It's false; you walk around looking suspiciously at the sky, sure that any minute now all snowy hell will break loose. But people started wearing light coats and sat with their faces to the sun in parks on the still-damp benches. Horse-drawn carriages were full of smiling tourists, and I knew when they got home they'd rave about Vienna and its marvelous winter weather.

The one thing I did like about it was the change it brought in India. She was suddenly gay and full of life again. Although my longing for Karen deepened by the day, being around India again reminded me why I had been so attracted to her from the beginning. At her best, she radiated a supremely clever and interesting life-view that made you want to know her opinion on everything. Whether it was a painting by Schiele or the difference between Austrian and American cigarettes, what she had to say made you either sit up and take notice or else hate yourself for never having had the intelligence or imagination to see it that way yourself. So many times I wondered what would have happened to us if I hadn't met Karen. But I had, and she now monopolized my capacity to love.

I thought about her constantly and, mustering my courage one Saturday night, called her in New York. While the phone rang, I moved through her apartment in my mind, an affectionate camera stopping here and there to focus in on things I liked or felt particularly nostalgic about. She wasn't in. I feverishly figured out the time difference and felt a little better when I realized I'd miscalculated—it was only a little after one in the afternoon there. I tried again later, but still no answer. It made me groan with doubt and jealousy; I knew if I called again and she wasn't there, my heart would break. I called India instead and asked in a sad voice if she wanted to go to the movies.

When we got to the theater we discovered the film didn't start for fifteen minutes; I was all for taking a slow walk around the block to kill time. When I moved to go, India took my arm and held me there.

"What's up?"

"I don't want to go tonight."

"What? Why?"

"Don't ask why, I just don't want to go, okay? I changed my mind."

"India—"

"Because this theater reminds me of Paul, all right? It reminds me of the night we all met here. It reminds me of—" She whirled around and walked away. She stumbled once and then strode forward, widening the gap between us with every step.

"India, wait! What are you doing?"

She kept moving. Trying to catch up with her, I noticed out of the corner of my eye an ad in a travel agency window for a trip to New York.

"India, for godsake, will you stop!"

She did, and I almost bumped smack into her. When she turned, the tears on her face shone, reflecting the white lights from a store window. I realized I didn't want to know why she was crying. I didn't want to know what new thing I had done wrong, or in what new way I had failed her.

"Can't you see he's everywhere in this town? Everywhere I turn, everything I see . . . Even *you* remind me of him."

She was off again, with me trailing after her like a bodyguard.

She crossed a couple of streets and entered a small park. It was dimly lit; a bronze statue in the middle was our only companion. She stopped, and I stood facing her back a few feet away. Neither of us moved for some time. Then I saw the dog.

It was a white boxer. I remember someone once telling me that breeders often kill white boxers when they're born because they're freaks, mistakes of nature. I sort of liked them and enjoyed seeing such funny yet brutal faces the color of clouds.

The dog came from nowhere and gleamed, a moving patch of snow in the night. It was alone and had no collar or muzzle on. India hadn't moved. I watched it sniff its way over to us. When it was only a few feet away, it stopped and looked directly at us.

"Matty!" She sucked in breath and grabbed my arm. "It's Matty!"

"Who? What are you talking about?" The tone of her voice made me scared, but I had to know what she was saying.

"It's Matty. Matterhorn! Paul's dog in London. We gave him away when we moved here. We had to because— Matty! Matty, come here!"

He started moving again: in the bushes, on the walk, across the flower bed. In the dark he glowed and moved busily, doing dog's business. He was huge. He must have weighed over eighty pounds.

"Matty! Come!" She bent down. He came right toward her, wiggling and whimpering like a puppy.

"India, be careful. You don't know—"

"Shut up. So what?" She looked at me with eyes as mad as fire.

The dog heard the change in her tone of voice and stopped dead, two feet away. It looked at India and then at me.

"Matty!"

It lowered its head and growled.

"Go away, Joe, you're scaring it."

It growled again; only this time the sound was longer and deeper, far more feral and threatening. The lips curled back, and it began to wag its stump of tail too fast.

"Oh, God. *Joe?*"

"*Move back.*"

"Joe—"

I spoke in a quiet monotone. "If you go too fast, it'll come. Go slow. No, *slower.*"

She was in a squat, and it was almost impossible for her to move backward. For an instant I looked around for a branch or a stone I might use to hit it with, but there was nothing. If it came, I would have only my hands and feet; stupid, impossible weapons against the giant boxer.

India managed to move two or three feet. With all the courage I'd ever had in my life, I slowly slid over so that I was standing between India and the dog. It was growling continually now; I wondered if it was rabid. I didn't know what to do. How long would it stand there? How long would it wait? What did it want? The growl turned into a kind of snapping snarl, and it sounded as if something were hurting the dog from inside its body. It turned its head left and right, then widened and narrowed its eyes. If it was rabid and bit me . . .

I realized for the first time I was chanting, "Jesus Christ, Jesus Christ . . ." under my breath. I didn't dare move. My hands were splayed flat against the sides of my legs. My fear had turned into a thick, evil taste in the back of my mouth.

Someone whistled, and the dog snapped at me in a madness of fast little bites at thin air, but it stayed where it was and moved only when the whistle came a second time.

"Very good, Joey! You passed the Matty test! He passed, India!"

Paul stood at one edge of the park. He was wearing the Little Boy top hat, white gloves, and the most beautiful black overcoat I had ever seen.

The dog bounded up to him and jumped high at a hand Paul had raised in the air over his head. The two of them disappeared into the dark.

5

"Joseph?"

"Karen!"

"Hello, love. Is it okay to talk?"

"Sure, just let me sit down."

Karen. Karen was on the other end of the line, and Karen was the heaven that made everything right again.

"Okay, so tell me what's up? Tell me everything. I tried to call you."

"Hey, Joseph, are you okay? You sound as if you just got your teeth pulled."

"It's the connection. How are *you?*"

"I'm . . . I'm okay."

"What does that mean, okay? Now you sound as if all *your* teeth were pulled."

She laughed; I wanted the sound to go on forever.

"No, Joseph, I'm really fine. What's goin' on there? What's happenin' with that Miss India and you?"

"Nothing. I mean, nothing's going on. She's all right."

"And you?"

Oh, did I want to tell her. Oh, did I want her there with me. Oh, did I want this all to be over.

"Karen, I love you. I don't love India, I love you. I want to come back. I want you."

"Uh huh."

I closed my eyes and knew something awful was about to come. "What's with Miles, Karen?"

"You want the truth?"

"Yes." My heart raced to match the beat of the heart of a man about to be hanged.

"I've been stayin' with him. He's asked me to marry him."

"Oh, God."

"I know."

"*And?*" Don't say yes. God in heaven, don't say you said yes.

"And I told him I wanted to talk to you."

"He knows about me?"

"Yes."

"Do you want to marry him?"

"The truth?"

"Yes, goddamn it, tell me the truth!"

Her voice went cold, and I hated myself for snapping at her. "Sometimes I think I do, Joseph. Sometimes I do. What about you?"

Shifting in my seat, I banged my calf on the leg of the chair and nearly fainted from the pain. It clouded my mind badly, and I groped for something clear and right to say to stop the best thing in my life from going down the drain.

"Karen, can you wait before you tell him anything? Can you wait a little while longer?"

A silence followed that lasted a hundred years.

"I don't know, Joseph."

"Do you love me, Karen?"

"Yes, Joseph, but I might love Miles more. I swear to God, I'm not trying to be coy, either. I don't know."

I sat in my room and smoked. The radio was on, and I smiled bitterly when India's song from our night in the mountains, "Sundays in the Sky," came on. How long ago had that been? How long ago had I held Karen in my arms and sworn to myself I wouldn't go back to Vienna? Ever. Everything was in New York. Everything. But how close was I to losing it now?

As had happened several times, the face of a white boxer raced across my mind, followed by the sound of India screaming. I knew somewhere inside I should have felt proud for having saved her that night, but the experience only made things seem more futile. How do you defeat the dead? Do you tell them to fight fair, no tricks or crossed fingers behind their back? What good was it to put up your two dukes, only to discover your opponent had a hundred, and another hundred, waiting when the first ones tired. I asked myself if I hated India, and knew I didn't. I didn't even hate Paul. It was impossible to hate the insane—like being angry at an inanimate object after you've banged your elbow on it.

I heard the refrigerator click on in the kitchen. A horn beeped in the street. Some children in the building screeched and laughed and banged a door. I knew it was time to talk to India. I would stay and help her all I could, but in return she would have to know that, if Paul's siege ended, I would not stay with her any longer than I had to. It would hurt and confuse her, I knew, but my ultimate allegiance was to Karen, and I could not ask her in all good faith to wait for me so long as I was being dishonest with India. Before we hung up that night, Karen asked if I was staying in Vienna because I was India's friend or because I was her lover. When I said "friend," I knew it was time to start acting truthfully, all the way around.

I asked India to meet me at the Landtmann. She wore a moss-green loden coat that came down to her ankles and black wool gloves that suited her perfectly. What an attractive woman. What a hell of a mess.

"You're sure you don't mind being here, India?"

"No, Joe. They have the best cake in town, next to Aida, and I owe you at least two disgusting pieces after the other night.

"Remember the first night we met? How we sat out here and I complained about how hot it was?"

We stood with our backs to the door of the café. The

trees were bare; it was hard to imagine them in full bloom. How could nature shed its skin so completely and then recreate it so exactly only a few months later?

"What are you thinking about, Joey?"

"The trees in winter."

"Very poetic. I was thinking about the first night. You know what? I thought you were kind of nerdy."

"Thanks."

"A good-looking nerd, but a nerd."

"Why in particular, or just generally?"

"Oh, I don't know, but I forgave you because of your looks. You're very cute, you know."

If you want Vienna to live up to your romantic expectations, get off the plane and go directly to Café Landtmann. It is marble tables, velvet seats, floor-to-ceiling windows, and newspapers from every interesting part of the world. It is, to be sure, one of the places where people go to look at one another, but it's such a large café that even that doesn't matter.

We chose a table by a window and looked around a while before either said anything. When we did, it was at the same time.

"In—"

"Who was—"

"Go ahead."

"No, you go ahead, Joe. I was only going to blabber."

"Okay. Are you in the mood to talk? I want to tell you something important."

She bowed her head, giving me the floor. I had no idea if this was the proper time to bring up Karen Mack, but like it or not, I had to.

"India, when I was in New York, I was with someone."

"I kind of thought so by the way you've acted since you got back. Somebody old or somebody new?"

"Somebody new."

"Uh oh, they're the most dangerous kind, aren't they? Before you go on, tell me her name."

"Karen. Why?"

"Karen Why. Is she Chinese?"

Despite the heaviness of the moment, I cracked up. I shook my head and kept laughing. Then our cake came, and we compared whose was better and who'd gotten gypped with a smaller piece.

"So go on with Karen, Joe. She's not Chinese and she's new."

"Why did you want to know her name?"

"Because I like to know the name of the enemy before I charge."

I told her about it generally, and India didn't say a word until I'd finished.

"And you slept with her?"

"No, not yet."

"Spiritual." She took a fork and squashed half her cake down flat on her plate.

She wouldn't look at me when she spoke again. She kept attacking the cake. "Why did you come back?"

"Because you're my friend and because a lot of this is my fault."

"Any love in there, Joey?"

"How do you mean?"

"I mean, did any of your choosing to come back have to do with loving me?"

Her head was bent, and I saw the careful, exact part in her hair.

"Of course there was love, India. I'm not . . ."

She looked up. "You're not *what*?"

"I'm not a good enough person to have returned if I didn't love you. Does that make sense?"

"Yes, I suppose. What are my chances against her?"

I closed my eyes and rubbed my face with my hands.

When I took them away, I looked at her. She had the most astounded look on her face. She was gaping over my shoulder, and both hands were on the table, trembling. I turned around to see what was so amazing. Paul Tate, in his beautiful black overcoat, was making his way through the café to our table.

"Hello, *Kinder*, can I sit down?" He slid in next to his wife and kissed her hand. Then he reached over the table and touched me gently on my cheek. His fingers were warm as toast.

"It's been a long time since I was in here. Right before you went to Frankfurt, Joey." He looked around fondly.

It was Paul. It was Paul Tate. He was dead. He was sitting across the table from me, and he was dead.

" 'Men, you may wonder why I've gathered you all here today . . .' No, I won't be dumb now."

"Paul?" India's voice was the chiming of a small clock in a room miles away.

"Let me say what I have to say, love, and you'll understand everything." He smoothed his hair back with one brisk gesture. "You were right, by the way, India. Right all along. When I died I didn't know if it was because of my heart or because of what you two did to it. It doesn't matter. It's over. Now all of my stuff is done, too. All of the Boy, all of the birds and the white Mattys . . . Done. You two betrayed me once and that's unforgivable, but it was *because* you loved each other. Finally I'm convinced of that. I see it's true now."

Despite his presence, India and I snuck glances across the table to see how we were reacting to *that*. Especially in light of what we'd just been saying.

"I loved India and could *not* believe she'd done it. You see, Joe, she really is a true person, no matter how it looks now. You remember that. When she loves you, it's all yours. When I realized what had happened, I wanted to kill you both. Big irony—I died instead. Death wasn't what I thought it would be; I was given the chance to come back and get you guys, and I took it. Brother, did I take it! It was fun at first too, seeing you little bastards screech and run around, really scared. It was. Then, Joe, you kept protecting her. Sticking your neck out so far it should have been cut off ten times. You did everything right and loving, and after a while and a lot of pain, it struck home how much you loved her. You didn't have to come back from New York, but you did. The way you protected her from the dog the other night ... It showed me you loved her with everything you've got, and I was amazed. You passed the test, if you can call it that, with flying colors, Joey. You convinced even me. So no more Boy. No more of the dead, Goodbye."

He got up, buttoned his overcoat to the neck, and, with a quick wink for both of us, walked out of our lives.

One of the famous Lennox family stories goes like this: Right after my father's mother died, my mother made us all go on a picnic to Bear Mountain. She wanted to keep my father as busy as possible, and picnics were a favorite of his. Ross didn't want to go at the last minute, but after a slap and some whispered oaths from the boss, he behaved himself and ended up eating more fried chicken and potato salad than anyone else. When we were done, my father and I went for a walk. I was terribly worried about him and kept thinking of the right thing to say to ease his pain. I was five and there weren't many things I knew how *to* say, much less well, so when it came I was excited and proud that I had thought it up all by myself.

We sat down on a couple of tree stumps, and I took his hand in mine. Did I have something to tell him!

"Daddy? You know you shouldn't be so sad that Grandma's dead. You know why? Because she's with our Big Father now, the one who takes care of *evvveryone*. You know who that is, Daddy? He lives up in the sky and his name is D-O-G."

In the days that followed our meeting with Paul, I wondered where he was. If he'd told the truth, where did people go after they died? I now knew one thing for sure—there were choices on that other side of life; things were far more complex there than anyone could imagine. Never once when he was sitting with us had I thought to ask him about it, but afterward I realized he probably wouldn't have said anyway. I was sure of that. It was Paul's way.

D-O-G. I was sorry I'd never had the chance to tell him that story.

7

"Where's Paul's pen?"

She stood in the door of my apartment in a purple rage.

"Do you want to come in?"

"You took it, didn't you?"

"Yes."

"I knew it, you little thief. Where is it?"

"It's on my desk."

"Well, go get it."

"All right, India. Take it easy."

"I don't want to take it easy. I want that pen."

She followed me in. I felt stupid and guilty. Ten-year-old guilt. My head bulged with conflicting ideas and emotions. Paul was gone, but exactly what did that mean? I could go now; I had done my duty to India. When was anything ever that simple? I hadn't answered her question about whether or not she had a "chance" against Karen. If Paul had remained a factor in our lives, I wouldn't have had to answer that question for a long time. Now I did.

"Give me that! Why'd you steal it, anyway?" She shoved it into her pocket and patted it a couple of times to make sure it was there.

"I guess because it was Paul's. I took it right after he died, before anything started to happen, if it makes any difference."

"You could have asked, you know."

"You're right—I could have asked. Do you want to sit down or anything?"

"I don't know. I don't think I like you very much today. What are you planning to do now? What's on your agenda? You could have called me, you know."

"India, back off, huh. Slow down."

Karen in New York; a fifty-fifty chance I could win her back if I left immediately. India in Vienna; free, alone, angry. Angry because she had betrayed the true love of her life for me. Angry because she thought I had come back to her for all the best reasons in the world, only to find at the worst possible time I'd done it out of ninety percent duty and only ten percent love. Angry because her betrayal had caused death and pain and fear and finally, in the end, a future that promised little more than permanent guilt and self-hatred.

Looking at her, I knew all of that and, in an incredible instant of clarity, decided that no matter what happened I would stay with India as long as she needed me. A montage of Karen in bed, at the altar, raising and loving *his* children,

laughing forever at his jokes, came and went, and I told myself I had to believe it didn't matter anymore. India needed
me, and the rest of my life would be utterly false and selfish—inexcusable—if I failed her now.

It wasn't martyrdom or altruism or anything as lovely as
all that. I would simply be doing what was right for the third
or fourth time in my life, and that was good. I realized how
naïve and unrealistic people are to think you can be both
right and happy.

If it happens that way, you are truly one of the blessed.
Right, however, should win if you have to choose. A great
deal has happened since those thoughts paraded grandly
through my head, but I still believe that's true. It is one of
the few things I still believe at all.

"Joe, since you'll probably be leaving soon, I want to tell
you something. I've been wanting to tell you for a long time,
but I haven't. I think you should know, though, because it's
important, and no matter what happens with us, I still love
you enough to want to help."

"India, can I say something first? I think it might have
some bearing—"

"No, not until I've finished. You know me. Whatever you
say may take the wind out of my sails, and I'm mad enough
at you to let it rip, so just let me, okay?"

"Okay." I tried to smile, but she frowned and shook her
head. No smiles allowed. I sat back to let her blow her top,
knowing I had the ace up my sleeve the whole time. Was
she going to be surprised!

"This pen is part of it. I know why you wanted it. Because
it was Paul's, and you wanted it to remind you of Paul's
magic. Right? I understand. You're like that, Joe. You want
part of everyone's magic, but you're too damned wimpy at
heart to reach it the hard way, so you snitch Paul's pen,
make love to me—"

"India, for godsake!"

"Shut up. You make love to me . . . You even steal your

brother's life, put it down on paper, and make it into a million-dollar story. Okay, not a million dollars, but enough to keep you sitting pretty for the rest of your life. True? You're talented, Joe, no one is arguing that, but have you ever thought maybe your greatest talent is stealing other people's magic and using it for yourself? Here, I want to read you something."

I couldn't believe what she was saying. Stunned and hurt more than I'd ever been in my life, I watched as she pulled a slip of paper out of her back pocket.

"It's from the novelist Evan Connell. You know him? Listen a minute. 'Originals attract us for another reason, which goes all the way back to prehistoric belief in magical properties. If we own something original, whether it's a skull or a lock of hair or an autograph or a drawing, we think maybe we acquire a little of the strength or substance of whoever it belonged to or whoever made it.' "

She threw the paper on the coffee table and pointed a finger at me. "It's you in a nutshell, Joe, and you know it down deep inside. I've been trying like hell to figure it out. The only word I can think of is parasite. Not a bad parasite, but one just the same. The two people you've truly loved and admired in your life—Ross and Paul—so overwhelmed you with whatever kind of magic they had that you knew you had to have some of it. So you stole your brother's story after he was dead, and it worked! When Paul arrived, you stole his wife, you stole his *pen* . . . Do you get what I mean, Joseph? Jesus, why am I calling you Joseph? You know the only reason why you'll stay with me? Because I might still have some of his magic left, and you can't bear to be alone in the world without any. Or maybe you'll leave because your Karen has a fresh supply and she'll keep your tank filled. It's a bad way to put it, Joe, but you get exactly what I mean. I'm sorry to stab you with all this at one time, but it's the truth. That's all. I've had my say. Do you want to talk now?"

"No. I think you had better go."

"All right. Think about it. Think about it a lot. Before you come and punch me in the nose, tear it apart and put it back together again. I'll be at home."

She got up and left without another word.

I sat in the chair for the rest of the afternoon. I looked at the floor and out the window. How dare she! What hideous thing had I done to her to deserve those words? I'd simply been honest, and she'd returned the favor by cutting me in half with a dull razor blade. What if I had been totally honest with her? Told her I truly loved someone else but was going to stay with her because it was my duty rather than my desire. That was the first, scorched-ego part of the afternoon's thoughts. The part where I very much wanted to punch her in the nose for having the nerve to tell me ...

The truth? Had I been searching for that truth ever since the death of my brother, or running away from it as hard as I could? I picked up the paper with the Connell quote and read and reread it.

The sun crossed the sky, and the shadows through the venetian blinds followed it. I would allow her one thing—I had taken advantage of Ross's death, sure, but wasn't that what a writer was supposed to do? Cash in on his life's experience and try to make some sense of it on paper? How could she fault me for that? Would she have condemned me if the story hadn't happened in the right place at the right time? What if it had been an exercise for a creative-writing class in college and nothing more? Would that have been okay in her eyes?

She was jealous. Yes, that was it! All my fluke money and success from "Wooden Pajamas," being able to pull her away from Paul and then hinting I didn't want her after the danger had passed. She was a loser and I was a winner and ... Hard as I tried for a couple of minutes, I couldn't dress her in that outfit either. She wasn't the jealous type and certainly wouldn't wither up and blow away if I walked out of her life. There was a toughness in her that could weather all kinds of storms, and I wasn't egotistical enough to think my departure would bring the curtain down on her life. Pain and guilt, yes, but no final curtain.

Part Two in the revelations on a winter afternoon of one Joseph Lennox, writer and parasite.

When it grew dark outside, I walked without thinking into the kitchen and opened a can of soup. I have no memory from that point on, until I realized I'd just washed my dinner dishes. I zombied back to my thinking chair and sat down for the next installment.

Had my life, lucky as it was, run on automatic pilot from the day I'd pushed Ross until now? Was that possible? Could a person function in that kind of vacuum for so long without knowing it? It wasn't true. Look at all the work I'd done! All the places I'd visited, all the . . . the . . .

A light winked on in an apartment on the other side of the courtyard, and I knew what she'd said was right. Not exactly, because I knew it wasn't magic I was trying to suck from other people, but rather a delight in life I knew I'd never have.

A delight in life. That was what Ross and Paul Tate had in common, as did India and Karen. If magic was the thing, India had sold herself short by not taking her own into account. I *did* want what she and those other people had—the ability to live at ten out of ten on life's scale for as long as they possibly could. Me? I'd always chosen three or four, because I was afraid of the consequences of higher numbers.

Ross stuck his nose right in life's face and challenged it to constant duels. Paul and India jumped into it blindly, not ever worrying about what would happen to them, because no matter what, the results would be interesting. Karen went out and bought you cowboy boots because she loved you. She was awed by the light coming through a glass of red wine and cried at old movies because one *should* cry then.

A delight in life. I put my head in my hands and wept. I couldn't stop. I had done so many things wrong; judged distances and temperatures and hearts (including my own!) incorrectly from Day One, and now I knew why. I wept, and it didn't even feel good, because I knew I'd never have the delight they did; it tore me apart.

What could I do? I had to talk to India. I had to tell her all of this. I also wanted to tell her about Ross and what I had done to him. She was a good psychiatrist (a little off the mark, but not much, considering the things she didn't know!). Even if she thought I was using her again, I wanted her thoughts on what I should do, now that the cat was out of the bag; now that I had the rest of my life to live.

As I rubbed my nose on my sleeve, I started laughing. I remembered a ridiculous poster I'd seen in a head shop years before, which even then struck me as particularly trite and offensive: *Today is the first day of the rest of your life.* You could say that again.

"India? It's Joe. Can I come over and talk?"

"Are you sure you want to?"

"Very sure."

"Okay. Should I put on my boxing gloves?"

"No, just be there."

I took a shower and chose my clothes carefully. I wanted to look good, because I wanted it all to be good. I even put on a tie I'd been afraid to wear for a year because it had cost so much. When I was ready, I stood in the doorway and gave a quick look around the apartment. Everything was neat and tidy, in place. Maybe when I returned my life would be in place, too. I had a chance, a fighting chance, to set things right, and I was grateful.

I would have walked, but was so excited by all I had to say to her that I took a cab. As with the soup I'd eaten earlier, I was so preoccupied that I didn't realize we'd moved until the taxi pulled up at her door; the driver had to ask twice for eighty schillings. I got out the key she'd given me and let myself into the building. A smell of cold stone and dust was waiting, but I had no time for it and took the stairs to her apartment two at a time.

"Two-at-a-time. Two-at-a-time." I said it to match the cadence of my feet on the steps. Unconsciously I counted how many there were. I'd never done that before. Thirty-six. Twelve, then a landing; twelve, then a landing . . .

"Twelve-then-a-land*ing!*" I was out of breath, but so hyper by the time I got to her floor I was afraid I'd break her door down.

She preferred that I use my key to the apartment because every time I rang the bell she was either in the bathroom or taking a soufflé out of the oven. Inevitably, as soon as she opened the door and greeted me, the next moment she was off, flying down the hall—back to whatever she'd been tending when I buzzed. I let myself in and was surprised to see that all the lights were out.

"India?" I went into the living room, which was only dark shapes lit by the night-gray light from the windows. She wasn't there.

"India?" Nothing in the kitchen. Or the hall.

Puzzled both by the darkness and by the silence, I wondered if something had happened while I was coming over. It wasn't like her to do this. What was wrong?

I was about to turn on the lights when I remembered the bedroom.

"India?" The light from the street fell in stripes over the bed. From the doorway I could see her lying there, with her back toward me. She had no top on, and her naked skin was like soft, bright clay.

"Hey, what's up?" I stepped halfway into the room and stopped. She didn't move. "India?"

"Play with Little Boy, Joey."

It came from behind me. A familiar, beloved voice that sent a vicious, twisting chill down my spine. I was afraid to turn, but I had to. He was there. Little Boy. He was behind me. He was there.

I turned; Paul Tate stood leaning in the doorway, his arms crossed over his chest, the tips of white gloves showing behind his armpits. His top hat was cocked to one side. A dancer in the night.

I began to crouch like a child. There was nowhere to go. Lower. If I got lower, he wouldn't see me. I could hide.

"Play with Little Boy, Joey!" He took off his hat and, in a slow dream, peeled Paul Tate's face down and off his own: a smirking Bobby Hanley. "April Fool, scumbag."

"Joe?" India called from the bed and, a snake to the charmer's pipe, I turned.

She was facing me now, the light unnaturally bright over her naked form. She reached behind her head and, in a quick ripping motion, tore her hair and face away.

Ross.

Where the strength came from I don't know, but I sprang from my squat and, shoving Bobby aside, ran out of the apartment.

I was going so fast I slipped on the first steps and almost fell, but I grabbed the metal banister and righted myself. Out of the door to the street. Move, run; go, run.

What do I do? Where do I go? Bobby, Ross, Paul, India. My feet slapped those names at me as I ran nowhere, anywhere. Away. As fast as I'd ever run in my life. Move! A car honked, and I brushed its cold metal with my hand. A dog screamed because I kicked it running by. The owner's outraged cry. Another car horn. Where was I going? Ross. He'd done it.

Karen! Get to Karen! The idea lit my mind. A gift from God. Get to Karen! Get to New York. Run and hide, and go to Karen, where there was love and truth and light. Karen. She would save me. I looked fearfully over my shoulder for the first time to see if they were following me. They weren't. Why? Why weren't they there? It didn't matter. I thanked God for that, thanked him for Karen. I ran and prayed and saw it all—the whole Ross game. Saw it all with such perfect clarity that it was all I could do to keep myself upright. I wanted to lie down in the street and die. But there was Karen. She was sanctuary.

Things became clearer. I knew I was near an overhead station stop, and the train went near the Hilton Hotel. I could go to the Hilton and take a bus from there to the airport. Still running, I felt my back pocket to see if my wallet was there with all my money and credit cards. It was. Hilton, bus to the airport, first plane—*any* plane—out of Vienna, and then a connection from wherever to New York. To Karen.

Heaving for breath, I got to the station and once again took stairs two at a time.

No one was on the platform. I cursed because that probably meant a train had recently come and gone. I clenched and unclenched my fists at no trains, Ross, life. Ross was India. I had fallen in love with, made love to . . . my brother. How brilliant. Utterly fucking brilliant.

I paced up and down the platform, straining my eyes down the tracks, trying to will a train to appear. Then I looked behind me at the steps to see if anyone was coming. No one. Why? When that question began to frighten me, the thin line of a train light showed down the track. I was saved. As it grew larger, I heard someone coming up the stairs. The steps were slow and heavy, tired. The light loomed larger; the steps kept coming. The train snaked noisily into the station and stopped. The steps did too. The two cars in front of me were completely empty. I reached for the door and was about to pull it open when she spoke.

"Joseph?"

I turned; Karen was there. My Karen.

"Play with Little Boy!"

Ross.

EPILOGUE

Formori, Greece

There are one hundred people on this island. Tourists never come, because it is an ugly, rocky place and not what one has in mind when one thinks of Greece. Its closest neighbor is Crete, but that is seventeen hours away over the sea. With the exception of a supply boat that comes about every two weeks, we rarely see others. That is fine.

My house is stone and simple. Two hundred feet away is the water. I have a wooden bench by the door and I sit on it for hours. It is pleasant. I pay well, so they bring me lamb and fish to cook at the end of each day. Kalamaria, sometimes even great red lobsters big enough for three people. I sit outside when the weather is good, but fall is coming and there are many storms. They are brutal and endless. It doesn't matter. If it rains, I light a fire inside my house and cook and eat and listen to the rain and the wind. My house, my bench, the wind, the rain, the sea. I can trust them. I can trust nothing else.